GET THE AUDIOBOOK

jljarvis.com/sunlight-on-cedar-creek

ALSO BY J.L. JARVIS

Waterfront Summers

The Cottage at Peregrine Cove

The House on Serenity Lake

Moonlight on Mariner's Bluff

Drake & Wilde Mysteries

#1 *Love in the Time of Pumpkins*

#2 *Secrets in the Hollow*

#3 *Shadow of the Horseman*

Standalones

A Kiss in the Rain

App-ily Ever After

Once Upon a Winter

The Red Rose

Highland Vow

Short Stories

Seasons of Love: A Short Story Collection

The Eleventh-Hour Pact

A Christmas Yarn

The Farmer and the Belle

Work-Crush Balance

Cedar Creek

Christmas at Cedar Creek

Snowstorm at Cedar Creek

Sunlight on Cedar Creek

Pine Harbor

Allison's Pine Harbor Summer

Evelyn's Pine Harbor Autumn

Lydia's Pine Harbor Christmas

Holiday House

The Christmas Cabin

The Winter Lodge

The Lighthouse

The Christmas Castle

The Beach House

The Christmas Tree Inn

The Holiday Hideaway

Highland Passage

Highland Passage

Knight Errant

Lost Bride

Highland Soldiers

The Enemy

The Betrayal

The Return

The Wanderer

American Hearts

Secret Hearts

Forbidden Hearts

Runaway Hearts

For more information, visit jljarvis.com.

Get monthly book news at news.jljarvis.com.

SUNLIGHT ON CEDAR CREEK

SUNLIGHT ON CEDAR CREEK

J.L. JARVIS

SUNLIGHT ON CEDAR CREEK

Published by Bookbinder Press
bookbinderpress.com

ISBN (ebook) 978-1-942767-45-9
ISBN (paperback) 978-1-942767-46-6
ISBN (hardcover) 978-1-942767-49-7
ISBN (audiobook) 978-1-942767-50-3

ONE

The people who sat in unhurried contentment in coffee shops were not Zoey's people. But being unremarkable had its rewards. She could wind her way around all the sleekly styled furniture with its bright colors and curves and pass by their conversational groupings unnoticed and unscathed by nonverbal judgment.

The usual characters hovered in the periphery as though coffee shops were life's waiting rooms. In a dark corner, two weathered and ink-smudged hands clung to a daily newspaper. Both wrinkled skin and paper were relics of an era gone by. A few tables over, a young guy in short sleeves with a sticker-laden computer drummed at the keyboard. The old hands and clacking fingers framed two young lovers leaning over another small circular table. They wore tangled hair and creased clothes like a badge, and their foreheads practically touched as they shared a phone, a pair of earbuds, and intimate smiles.

Joining the line now three deep, Zoey gazed blankly ahead. Before her, a young mother stooped to retrieve a pacifier from the floor, licked it clean, then returned it to her fussing baby. Zoey winced and looked toward the window, where a high school–aged girl sat at a counter and stared outside with ennui.

Zoey's turn came. "Two coffees, please."

The barista stared with an odd combination of bored expectancy.

"Oh, sorry. Medium."

"Medium what?" He pointed to the columns of handwritten text on the large chalkboard menu.

Zoey furrowed her brow. "Two coffees. One black, one with cream and sugar."

The barista gestured to the condiment bar at the end of the line. "So just regular coffee?"

Zoey lifted her chin and nodded, offering an apologetic half smile. After paying, she sidled along to the waiting area at the end and glanced at her watch. She had enough time to make it to work, with a few minutes to spare. When her order was up, she added the cream and sugar herself, topped each cup with a lid, then headed for the door. She looked forward to a leisurely walk to work, sipping the hot liquid in the crisp morning air, the cool breeze gently tossing the tips of her sandy-blond bob.

As she reached for the door, it flung open.

"Oh!" Zoey took a reflexive step back yet still found herself face-to-face—or rather, face-to-chest—with a stranger. She lifted her eyes to meet his. Firm jaw, deep-blue eyes, and straight, uncombed black hair. *Hmm. Probably a tourist. Definitely attractive.* Their gazes locked for a moment.

He rallied first with a confident smile, took a step back, and pushed open the door. He gestured for Zoey to pass underneath his long, sturdy arm.

"Thank y-you." Her words came out in hoarse, broken tones. She inhaled his scent as she ducked under his arm. *Is that deodorant or soap?* Whatever it was smelled good. She hadn't been so close to a man in a long time. Heat rushed to her cheeks. *Please don't see me blushing.*

She left quickly, but not before a backward glance to catch sight of his apparent amusement. *Ugh.*

Tossing aside her original plan, Zoey sped up. She tried to ignore the familiar sick, anxious feeling that now gripped her chest.

Soon, she made it to the back of the Cedar Creek Opera House, an old vaudeville house her great-grandfather had won playing poker. With a good business sense coupled with his life's savings, he'd converted it to a movie theater, and the business had gotten the family through the Depression. After that, family lore built it into something lucky. They'd passed it down until it fell into Aunt Minnie's hands.

An outsider might look at the threadbare seats and moth-eaten velvet stage curtains and see little more than a nostalgic money pit. But for Aunt Minnie, it was her legacy. It might be on its last legs, but she would never sell.

Buoyed by townspeople who revered it as a treasured local landmark and her aunt's dogged resourcefulness, she kept it afloat. Fridays and Saturdays were vintage movie nights unless the local community theater troupe was in residence. On Sundays, a small church rented the space for its weekly worship services. During the week, the lobby catered to tourists and weekenders as a gallery and gift shop featuring the work of local artists. The combined revenue barely covered the bills with enough to set aside for the annual property taxes.

As Zoey walked in through the stage door, her mind lingered on the brief coffee shop encounter. He'd looked about her age, pushing thirty, although his confident air had made him seem older. If he was her age, then he wasn't a local. She would have remembered him from Cedar Creek High. People changed after high school, but no one she knew had changed that much.

Zoey sighed. *Look at me, fixating on some random guy in a coffee-shop doorway. I must be really lonely.* She chided herself. After all, she was only human. She might be an anxiety-ridden quasi-agoraphobe, but she still had eyes. *He's exactly my type.* Tall with strong features and defined shoulders, he was probably most people's type. And he'd held the door for her, but that had probably just been self-preservation.

Had she arrived one second sooner, she would have bumped into him, doused his lumberjack-plaid shirt with not one but two cups of scalding coffee. Or his jeans. She winced at the thought. Her mind wandered. *His jeans...* It had happened too fast to get a good look at those. Now, that was a shame.

"Good morning!"

That time, Zoey did nearly spill the coffee. She coughed as Aunt Minnie set a box down on the concession counter.

Poor Aunt Minnie had the misfortune of an ironic name. Her parents hadn't anticipated how uncommonly tall she would become. Then again, she'd had over sixty years to adjust to the name. Besides, everyone in town knew her, so Zoey imagined by then it must be a nonissue.

"Good morning!" Zoey grinned and held out the other coffee.

"Thank you. Just what I needed." Minnie's eyes lit with the warmth that had always made Zoey feel safe despite all that had happened. "Today marks one week on the job. What do you think?"

"What do I think? I think I'm grateful!"

Her aunt must have seen Zoey's eyes misting up, because she shrugged it off and blew air through her lips. "So you'll stay?"

"Yes, of course—if you'll have me."

Aunt Minnie waved off her remark. "Have you? I'm delighted you're here. You're doing me a great favor."

Zoey looked past her aunt's kind assurances. "Thank you for taking me in."

Aunt Minnie held out her arms and gave her a hug. "Don't be silly. We're family."

But she was taking her in and not for the first time. When Zoey had lost both her parents to a plane crash, Aunt Minnie had driven down to Tarrytown, settled things there, and brought Zoey home with her to Cedar Creek.

"I'm so glad you're here." Aunt Minnie's eyes crinkled as a broad smile creased her face. She sighed. "Well, I've got some errands to run. You remember how to handle the register?"

Zoey gave her a confident nod. She had worked there part-time through high school and during vacations from college. In those years, she had taken tickets, run the concession stand, and climbed the dimly lit stairs to the projection booth, where she'd threaded spools of film through the projector and spliced the occasional broken bits back together. Late at night, she would linger after the last customer left and clean the sprockets with a toothbrush and a spray bottle of rubbing alcohol.

"Good," Aunt Minnie said. "If anyone comes in,

all the merchandise is barcoded. But if anything comes up, I've got my phone."

"I'll be fine."

"I know you will." With that, her aunt left.

Zoey looked around. Aunt Minnie had done an impressive job of converting the lobby into an art gallery and gift shop. She had cleverly displayed all the merchandise on racks with wheels, which were easily rolled into a locked storage area when the space was rented out.

Zoey tidied up the counter then took an empty box to the alley out back. She had just come back inside and closed the door behind her when a loud knock sounded. Her aunt must have forgotten something. She swung open the stage door and gasped. Instead of her aunt, there stood the guy from the coffee shop, looking equally startled.

His mouth spread to that same smile as he looked into her eyes. "Hello again."

"Hi." Her eyebrows furrowed. She couldn't manage to smile as easily as he did. "Sorry. I was expecting someone else."

"No problem." He walked past her and into Aunt Minnie's office.

Hold on. Zoey followed him. "Excuse me! Can I help you?"

"No, I'm good."

Zoey stared, slack-jawed, but couldn't seem to

find words. She was too distracted by the nervous fluttering in her stomach.

She arrived at the office and met him in the doorway as he turned to come out.

"Have you seen Minnie?"

"She stepped out."

His eyebrows knitted together. "Oh." He glanced back, returned to the filing cabinet, then lifted the sweater draped over the top to reveal a power drill. "There it is."

Zoey frowned. He seemed to have made himself a little too at home for a hired handyman. Zoey straightened her posture and parked herself in the doorway, blocking his exit. "Was she expecting you?"

"Yeah." He lifted the drill. "But I've got what I needed." He looked down at her and smiled.

Not only did his smile disarm her, but the butterflies in her stomach took flight to her chest. She stepped aside, hoping she'd done so before revealing how flustered she felt. It was different when he was just some guy in the coffee shop that she could look at and even admire. But now that he was a walking, talking person making himself at home in her aunt's theater, she didn't know how to react. To compound matters, he seemed completely at ease, which only highlighted her discomfort.

He headed for the storage room.

Zoey pulled out her phone and texted her aunt. *There's a guy here acting like he owns the place.*

An answer came back almost immediately. *Young, dark-haired, good-looking guy—a cross between Montgomery Clift and Gregory Peck?*

Zoey typed, *Who?*

Oh... a cross between Tom Sturridge and Theo James?

Yeah. I guess.

Aunt Minnie wrote, *His name's Tyler. Tell him I'm on my way.*

Zoey went to the storage room and called inside, "Hey, what's your name?"

He popped into the doorway, a bucket of assorted supplies in one hand, a toolbox in the other, and the power drill under his arm. "Tyler."

"Okay." Zoey looked up from her phone. "Aunt Minnie's on her way."

"No worries. I'll just get started."

He had gentle eyes, but they weren't enough to put Zoey at ease. Although the theater was well within her comfort zone, interacting with strangers was one of her issues. Good-looking ones made it worse.

Tyler took a step forward and stopped. "Would you grab that?" He nodded toward the coffee cup he'd left sitting on a shelf.

Zoey didn't react quickly enough to say no, so she watched him walk past and was forced to pick up the cup and follow. He stopped at the foot of the carpeted stairs that led up to the theater balcony.

Feeling uneasy and somewhat annoyed, she waited, coffee in hand, while he set everything down. Just when she was ready to gripe about not being his assistant, he straightened and took the coffee.

"Thanks." He flashed her another smile.

If she was going to get stupid every time he used that winning smile on her, there was only one thing to do. Leave.

Zoey headed back to the office. She stopped inside the doorway. *Exhale-two-three-four. Hold-two-three-four. Inhale-two-three-four. Hold-two-three-four.*

She continued to her aunt's chair to wait for her return, but when Zoey rounded the desk corner, there he was, in the doorway. He had followed her back.

"Is something wrong?" He looked genuinely concerned.

That gave her pause. *Do I look like something's wrong?* Panic shot through her. *The breathing exercises. He heard them.* Realizing her fixed gaze must give her a deer-in-the-headlights countenance, she glanced away. "No. Everything's fine."

His eyes softened, and he looked down as though he were at fault. Then his face lit with a revelation, and he grinned. "You must be Zoey!"

Thoroughly confused, she said, "Yes?"

He extended his hand. "Tyler Farrington."

She shook it, all the while hoping her palm wasn't too sweaty. "Zoey Beckett. Oh, right. You knew that."

TWO

Tyler's expression brightened. "So you're Minnie's Zoey." He gazed at her as though she were a fascinating museum specimen. Apparently realizing he still held her hand, he let go and offered a self-deprecating smile that was too charming by half. "Good to meet you."

"You too." She exhaled then hoped her relief hadn't been too obvious to him. When enough moments had passed to be subtle about it, she surreptitiously slipped her hand behind her and wiped her moist palm on her jeans.

"So, you're home for a visit?"

"Not exactly. I've moved back, actually." Aunt Minnie must not have told him.

He appeared genuinely interested. "From New York? That's quite a change."

"Yes, it is. But this is home. I feel safe and

comfortable here." *Safe and comfortable? That sounds weirdly revealing.*

Tyler barely moved, but Zoey saw in his eyes that her poor choice of words hadn't escaped his notice.

As though picking up on her discomfort, he attempted to make her words sound normal. "This town has that effect, don't you think? I mean, I'm not even from here, but I feel the same way. It's like the hometown you wish you'd come from."

That was exactly how she felt about Cedar Creek. Aside from a couple of unpleasant high school incidents, she loved it there and had from the start. For a moment, curiosity overcame her social anxiety, and she peered into his steady gaze. The warmth in his eyes was the sort one might get from a friend.

Her anxiety eased somewhat. She couldn't explain why, but he made her feel like he saw her worry yet didn't mind it at all. It was almost as if she could be herself with him. She chided herself again. That was wishful thinking on her part. She was attracted to him. That was all this nonsense was about.

Zoey exhaled. "Yeah, Cedar Creek's great." *Yeah, great. Well, Zoey, aren't you fascinating?* There it was again—that anxious feeling.

He nodded. A long pause followed. "Well, you must have work to do. Don't let me keep you." He flashed a warm smile and turned to lay out a drop cloth.

Zoey's eyebrows drew together. *Hey, wait a minute. Did he just give me the bum's rush? In my aunt's theater?*

Aunt Minnie's voice rang out and filled Zoey with relief. "Tyler! How are you?"

He looked up, walked over to her aunt, then gave her a warm hug.

Those two seem awfully chummy.

Zoey went to the concession counter and crouched down to tidy the shelves. They were chatting like old friends. *The weather. Hiking trails?* Apparently, Aunt Minnie knew some spots from back in the day. Zoey wasn't even sure how they got onto books.

Tyler said, "Yeah, I'm about tenth on the library wait list for that one."

"Oh, I just finished it," her aunt said. "I'll bring you my copy tomorrow."

"Thanks!"

They had a chatty tête-à-tête over the to-do list Tyler pulled from his pocket. He glanced up the curved stairway at the stained walls and chipped plaster. "Well, I'd better get to work on this."

Zoey arched an eyebrow. Despite his apparent affinity for tools, she hadn't gotten a repairman vibe from him at all. His hands were too smooth and his nails too even. She'd noticed when he set down his coffee a few minutes before. Those were the hands of a guy with a desk job. Or maybe he just had some incredible work gloves.

The more pressing question was how Aunt Minnie was going to pay for his work. Zoey hadn't looked at the books lately, but there had never been money for extras. There was barely enough for needed repairs like overflowing toilets or shorted electrical circuits. Zoey had already decided to pick up some repair skills of her own. The nearby community college taught continuing education classes, and the hardware store sometimes offered how-to workshops. But once Tyler started setting up, it was clear that Zoey's future skills were no match for him and his toolbox. He seemed to know what he was doing.

That sort of knowledge cost money. Zoey adored her aunt, but the woman was a dreamer. Her rich imagination had served her well for envisioning multiple income generators for the theater, but it might not prove as effective for her checkbook. Zoey felt she had to intervene.

As her aunt headed back to her office, Zoey pulled her aside. She whispered, "Let me save you some money. I've looked up some DIY classes. There's a lot I could do around here so you won't have to use people like him." She cast a sideways glance at Tyler, who was drilling holes in the plaster across the lobby.

Her aunt's face lit up. "Good! With the three of

us working, we'll have the place spruced up in no time."

"I meant—"

Aunt Minnie called out, "Tyler! Meet your new apprentice."

"What? No—"

Aunt Minnie hooked her arm and led her to Tyler. "She's a hard worker."

That's not what I meant. Zoey tried to think of a graceful way to get out of it.

Tyler grinned, no doubt amused by Zoey's panicked expression. "Good. Grab that vacuum, and let's get to work."

Still confused, Zoey glanced at her aunt then bent down to pick up the vacuum hose.

Aunt Minnie waved. "You two have fun. I've got some paperwork to do."

Before she could ask why, Tyler started to drill. Zoey heaved a sigh and followed him, vacuuming the holes as instructed. Then he told her to spray two squirts from a spray bottle into the holes.

This time, she was quick to ask, "Why?"

He looked up from his toolbox. "Because."

That's sound logic.

Next was caulking and screwing plastic disks into the wall. Tyler seemed to know what he was doing. Zoey wanted to ask what it was and why, but since Tyler was on the clock, each question would only cost Aunt Minnie more. Zoey resolved to spend some time watching online videos later. She would figure it out. After all, the theater had an endless supply of cracked plaster to fix. She would be ready to work solo in no time.

In the meantime, there was the matter of the handyman. The theater was a gold mine for him. He could put six children through college with the work the place needed. *Does he have children? A wife? Girlfriend? Possessive stalker?*

She refocused. "Look, Tyler, I know I must look like... whatever I look like." *Timid? Socially awkward?* "But Aunt Minnie means everything to me. I know how you tradesmen are. I get it. You're just making a living. But it comes at a cost." She glanced toward the office. The next part was hard to get out. "Whatever it is, it's too much."

She couldn't get a good read on his expression, so she made it clearer. "We can't afford you."

No matter how attractive you are with your tousled, arrow-straight dark hair and strong shoulders. She started daydreaming about the feeling of those arms of his on a cold winter's night. Or summer's. All the seasons, really. *And this is what being alone for years does to you. But it's okay. It's only in your mind.*

"What?" He looked stunned.

She expected that reaction. Guilt, maybe. That would have made sense. Or, giving him the benefit of the doubt and assuming he had no idea her aunt couldn't afford it, he might feel indignant. Her heart sank. Her moment of courage had passed. It wasn't guilt. He was clearly offended.

He set his caulk gun down and turned with a look that bored through her. "I'm just helping out. I've got some time, and your aunt could use a hand."

She pressed on. "Doesn't matter. Union, nonunion—she still can't afford you."

"Oh, I think she can afford free."

Free?

Ignoring Zoey's disbelief, he returned to drilling holes. "Now, back to work. Daylight's burning, and I charge time-and-a-half for overtime."

"But... right." She studied him. "Why?"

"I was kidding about the overtime. That would be zero."

She shook her head. "I mean, why are you doing this?"

"Do you really need to ask? Look around. There's enough work here for a large crew."

"But why you?"

He seemed taken aback. "Why not me? She needs help. I can help her." He shrugged as if it were perfectly logical.

He had to have some sort of angle. She couldn't think of one at the moment, so she said, "Thank you." That sounded weaker than she'd intended, but she was still deciding whether to take his kindness at face value.

She added, "I'm sorry if I misjudged you." *If. Which is not to say that I did—only that it's possible.*

With a sideways glance and a shrug, Tyler got back to work.

Two hours later, Aunt Minnie appeared. "There are sandwiches in my office if anyone's hungry."

Tyler called out, "I'll be there in a minute." Turning to Zoey, he said, "Go ahead. I just want to get the rest of the plaster on this section of wall."

"Okay." Zoey wiped her hands on a shop towel and left.

AUNT MINNIE WAS SETTING the conference table in her office for lunch when Zoey arrived.

"Tyler's on his way. He had to put some finishing touches on the plaster."

"Oh, good."

While they unwrapped Aunt Minnie's homemade sandwiches and poured drinks, Minnie said, "Tyler's nice, isn't he?" She raised an eyebrow. "And single."

Ignoring the last bit, Zoey proceeded with caution. "Well, considering the fact that I've only just met him, he seems nice enough."

"Nice enough to help around here for free."

Zoey finished putting napkins next to the plates and sat down. "Yeah, I was wondering about that.

People don't just do things for free. There's always an angle."

Aunt Minnie raised her eyebrows. "You're awfully young to be so cynical."

Not wanting to stir up a debate, Zoey said, "I guess life in the city has gotten to me."

Tyler walked in. "Life in the city gets to some people."

Zoey bristled. After spending a morning with Tyler, she was feeling slightly more comfortable with him—enough so to say, "Don't make assumptions. You've only just met me."

He raised an eyebrow. "What made you think I was talking about you?"

That caught Zoey off guard. "Well, because I'm the one who said it."

Aunt Minnie watched them like a tennis spectator at Wimbledon.

Tyler scratched the back of his neck. "Actually, I was thinking about *my* time in the city."

"Oh." Zoey felt like she ought to say more, but she drew a blank.

An awkward moment passed before Minnie cheerily said, "Why don't we sit down?"

Tyler appeared to shed any tension he felt from the exchange and took a seat. "Minnie, if you keep feeding me like this, I might keep coming back 'til you run out of repairs."

Aunt Minnie laughed. "We're a few lunches away from that point."

Zoey was halfway through her sandwich before she mustered the courage to speak. "So, Tyler..."

He turned a steady gaze on her.

She didn't think he meant anything by it. He just had such piercing blue eyes. But the damage was done. She was flustered. "So, well, I just wondered..."

Her aunt gave her that familiar look of concerned encouragement.

"What brings you to Cedar Creek?" Zoey exhaled, thankful she'd gotten something coherent out.

"I came up from the city, like you. But my first visit was just for the weekend. There's a bike shop here that does mountain bike tours."

Aunt Minnie said, "Oh, I didn't know you were a cyclist."

Tylor chuckled. "I'm not. A friend of mine is, and he dragged me along. I had a good time, but it wasn't really my thing. But Cedar Creek was. I kept dreaming about living here, then I just made it happen. What about you, Minnie?"

"Me? I've always loved Cedar Creek."

"No, I meant biking. Mountain or road bike?"

That drew a laugh from Aunt Minnie. "Even in my young and fit days, I was more of a ballet kind of girl."

He lifted his eyebrows and nodded, impressed. "I

can see it—you all covered in feathers, dancing gracefully across a large wooden stage."

Aunt Minnie's eyes twinkled. "I would have made a better lake than a swan. But I loved taking classes. I'll have you know, my teacher said I had an excellent turnout."

Tyler winked. "I'll bet you did."

Zoey leaned back in her chair and observed. *What the heck? He is shamelessly charming my aunt!*

"What about you, Zoey?" He peered at her.

"What?" He had a way of always catching her off guard.

"Do you like to ride bikes?"

She thought she detected a mischievous glint in his eyes. "Yeah, my trike's parked out back."

His mouth spread to a broad grin before stuffing the rest of the sandwich into it. Between bites, he said, "No, really."

"I'm a highly experienced walker. I've been doing it since I was one."

The corners of his mouth twitched, but he didn't crack a smile. "Really? Me too."

He was up to something, but she wasn't about to give him the satisfaction of falling into his trap—until he turned to her, looking entirely sincere, and said, "We should go walking sometime."

What is this, some nineteenth-century ritual like courting or something? Because that would be crazy. She was too stunned to speak.

Tyler's eyes darted about then he cast a questioning look at Aunt Minnie. She nodded slightly, urging him to continue.

They're working together? Zoey's anxiety spiked again when, with no warning, her aunt stood, made an excuse about having to go make a phone call, and left.

"Don't tell me—you just gave up walking." He smiled, but it didn't reach his eyes.

"I walked here from the coffee shop, didn't I?"

His eyebrows drew together. "Yes... but I just thought you might know of some good hiking trails around here."

"I'm not much of a hiker." Zoey was making things worse. She knew that. She was so well practiced, it was almost reflexive. He was asking her out, sort of. It wasn't dinner, but it was going somewhere together, which felt very datelike. He was smooth—asking her out as friends with no expectations. Then, if she passed, he might ask her out again. If not, no harm, no foul.

Zoey got it. She had dated enough. That was what held her back now. She had nothing against Tyler—quite the opposite. But her anxiety was always worse in social settings, and there was no more heightened social setting than a date. She wasn't about to put herself through the angst of all the developmental stages of a relationship when there was no point.

Zoey had ruined every relationship she'd ever had —not that there were that many. In the past, it'd felt more accidental. For the few that lasted, they eventually wanted some sort of commitment, and she couldn't bring herself to give it to them. It wasn't a conscious decision. There was just something inside her that couldn't go that extra step. Couldn't let go. After a while, it was easier not to bother. It would only end in discomfort, disappointment, or sometimes even tears—and maybe not just hers.

Dating in general pained her. Memories flashed through her mind. There had been the first dates that had also been the last. The worst one had been with a guy she was crazy about. He was so handsome, and he really seemed to like her. She got into his car and folded her arms. He asked if she was cold. She wasn't. She was just nervous. Things relaxed over dinner. Once she got used to people, she sometimes could talk. There were stretches where she felt like herself. He was so smart, successful, and interesting—the kind of guy she could've fallen in love with. At the end of the evening, he walked her to her door and asked if he could kiss her. The anxiety hit her like a big-wave surfer's wipeout. There was too much emotion. She couldn't handle it. She didn't want to lose it in front of him. So she'd simply said no.

He'd never asked her out again. Maybe if she'd explained that she just needed time, he might have understood. But she never gave him the chance.

There was one guy she had actually said yes to. Correct answer. His kiss did not disappoint. They were together for a couple of weeks. Then one morning, she woke up. He was gone. No note. No parting text. Just gone—with her last bagel.

When she'd stopped crying, she wondered if there might be some explanation. Maybe he'd come to the city for work and the job had ended. He'd gone home to his wife. Zoey preferred to imagine he'd been hit by a car on the way to the Empire State Building. Or anywhere. Then she felt guilty and imagined him making a complete recovery in the hospital with his dutiful wife by his side. She'd just flown in from Peoria. She was missing a tooth.

Tyler studied her as she ruminated. "Not a hiker. Okay." He smiled, but it was forced. "Well, I guess we'd better get back to work."

Zoey pushed back her chair and rose from the table. "I got this."

While she cleared the plates, Tyler walked out. "See you back at the wall."

THREE

Not even the shrill buzz of the drill could drown out Tyler's thoughts. Zoey Beckett had just shot him down worse than any woman he'd ever asked out. He considered himself to be fairly perceptive. If he'd have picked up any nonverbal cues that said, *Leave me alone*, he wouldn't have asked her out in the first place. And he still thought hiking and walking were pretty innocent activities. It wasn't as if he'd asked her out to dinner at a fancy restaurant where the pressure was on to dress up and be on her party manners.

Tyler glanced down at Zoey, who was engrossed in inserting adhesive into the holes he'd just drilled. He wished he could figure her out, but he couldn't infer much from his view of the top of her head. She was task oriented, diligent, and she didn't like him. *Simple as that.* But he liked her.

For the rest of the afternoon, the two plastered in relative silence. They even fell into a sort of rhythm. They worked well together, which seemed odd under the circumstances. By the end of the day, Tyler packed up and convinced himself that the minor bump in the road at lunch would be forgotten—by Zoey, at least.

Tyler brushed the debris off his hands and grinned at Aunt Minnie. "See you tomorrow." He cast a quick glance at Zoey and lifted his chin. It was almost a nod but with no eye contact. He left.

Tyler drove down the private dirt road that led to his cabin. He owned enough of the land from the main road back that he wouldn't have to see another human from his cabin or the creek that cut through his property. He liked it that way. As he stepped down from his truck, the tension left his shoulders.

Once inside, he looked around to admire his work. He'd just finished renovating the old one-room hunting cabin. Although he'd hired pros for some jobs like electrical and plumbing, he'd handled most everything else on his own. He ripped out the old Formica counters and floors in the kitchen, installed cabinets, and hand-poured and polished the concrete counters and island to match. The old fireplace had crumbled in spots. He'd tried but had needed to call in a stonemason for those repairs. After that, he added a wood stove for heat. The bathroom was a gut job, so once the plumbing was roughed out, he rebuilt it. An overstuffed leather sofa and chair by the fireplace finished the look. For the past several years, he'd lived the wandering life of a foreign correspondent and dreamed of the place. Now it was his.

He grabbed a beer from the fridge and went out to the porch to sit and watch the setting sun's rays dance on Cedar Creek. The relentless journey of the water had flattened the rocks in the creek bed, giving the appearance of shimmering plateaus. The timeless movement of water was soothing, but it was the sound that drove his troubles away. The creek's bubbling brought him sheer contentment.

One step away from being a recluse, Tyler enjoyed the solitude. But he'd gotten to a point where he would like to share it with someone. He'd never expected to feel that way. For the first few years, he had thrived as a nomad. He'd even loved the danger of it. Living life on the edge had been exciting—until it was real. People had died in those dangerous places. He'd watched them.

Setting the dark thoughts aside, he remembered the good times. Back then, he hadn't been looking for meaning. Relationships had been more about making contact—nothing deep, just a moment of closeness to satisfy an innate need for intimacy without the investment.

Tyler took a swig of beer. *I must be getting old. It's not enough anymore.* He kicked himself when his thoughts wandered back to Zoey. He was wasting his time trying to figure her out. He didn't get her. But maybe that was why he liked her. She didn't want him, so he had to have her. *It's Psych 101. Classic. And pathetic.*

But Zoey had struck a chord with him. She had something akin to his wandering spirit, but hers stemmed from a life lived apart. Beneath her slightly nervous facade, he sensed she was an observer. Her perceptions were deep if unexpressed. He wanted to know what went on in that head of hers and, even more, in that heart.

The warmth of the sun was long gone, so he finished his beer and went back inside. But he couldn't shake his longing to know Zoey Beckett.

THE NEXT DAY, Zoey continued to patch up the plaster with Tyler. While he plastered over the section of wall they had prepped, she went back and sanded the dry sections. Pausing to give her arm a break, she sat on a carpeted step and took a swig from her water bottle. She looked up and surveyed the cavernous theater lobby.

Tyler sat down beside her. She flinched.

"Sorry. I didn't mean to sneak up on you."

"That's okay." Or it would be when her heart slowed down to normal. She tried to do her four-beat breathing exercise without being obvious and focused on the wall.

He followed her gaze. "We'd have to get scaffolding and a crew of professionals to do a proper job of it."

Zoey nodded and exhaled her four-beat count, having had the same thought moments before.

"But at least we can freshen up the eye-level portions."

She looked at the next section of wall they needed to tackle. Even the touch-up job seemed like more than two people could handle. Tyler was awfully optimistic. Zoey asked, "Have you done very much of this sort of work?"

Tyler took a drink from his water bottle and set it down. "I used to help my dad do DIY projects on the house. And I just finished redoing my cabin."

Zoey took a breath. She'd almost said she would like to see it, which would have been a disaster. "Oh, what did you do?"

His face lit up with a mixture of pride and relief, no doubt because the work was done. "'What didn't I do' might be an easier question."

"Oh?"

"It was an old hunting cabin I got mainly for the cost of the land—ten acres. It's not huge, but it's big enough that I don't have to see anyone else unless I want to."

"That sounds nice."

"Does it? Some people hear that and suspect I'm a crazed recluse or fugitive from the law hiding out in the wild."

"Are you?" She tried to look serious but cracked a smile.

"No, I'm not nearly as interesting as that."

Zoey thought for a moment. "I've considered getting a place more remote."

"So you live here in town?"

"On the edge of town. In my aunt's house." She smirked. "Yeah, that's me. Life on the edge."

Tyler chuckled and eyed her a little too closely. "I bet you have your moments."

She gave him a sideways glance. "You'd lose that bet. I really like the idea of a little cabin in the woods, but then I think about bears. They would terrify me."

"Out there in the world, it helps to have firearms."

"Oh, I know. But I'm scared of those too."

Tyler's face fell. "I'm sensing a theme here."

Zoey's stomach sank. Now she'd done it—revealed too much. With a sigh, she decided the damage was done. There was no turning back. "Yeah. It's an ongoing theme with me." She tried to act as though it wasn't too big of a deal, but one look in Tyler's eyes, and she saw he knew better.

Tyler studied her for too long. It might've been only a moment or two, but even that felt like too much. His eyes softened. "That's okay. If you ever come out for a visit, I'll protect you."

A pang of emotions seized her in the chest. She tried to convince herself he was just kidding. But his eyes were so clear and honest that he couldn't have been teasing. Still, she couldn't hold his gaze. Her eyes flitted away.

She let out a deep breath and stood. "Well, we'd better get back to work before the boss sees us." She forced a smile of her own and went back to her sanding.

For the next hour, Zoey managed to keep the topic off of her, which wasn't easy. But he seemed willing to talk about his work on the cabin, so she kept firing questions about that until she ran out.

"In retrospect," Tyler said, "I could have started from scratch, and it might have been easier. But it's done, and it's just what I wanted."

The cabin sounded perfect to Zoey—so much so that she had a nagging desire to see it. But after deflecting his dating attempt, it would feel weird to suggest it. Maybe it hadn't even been a dating attempt. She might have read too much into it. But she was beginning to wonder if she'd done the right thing. Tyler was nice. Really nice. And, of course, he was good-looking. There was no need to dwell on the obvious, but that wouldn't stop her.

The conversation reached a lull. While Tyler refocused his full attention on plaster, Zoey stole a few glances his way. He had strong shoulders and arms, but he didn't have Popeye arms like those guys who spent too much time lifting weights. From the sound of it, his cabin renovation had been as good as several weeks at the gym.

Zoey couldn't help but notice him bend down for more plaster. That was some excellent scenery—which she apparently was enjoying too much. Once, he stood and caught her looking his way. She snapped her head in the other direction so fast, she feared she'd pulled a muscle. She blushed and dug into her sanding with renewed vigor.

The daylight through the windows was fading when Aunt Minnie called out, "It's past quitting time, you two. Maybe I need to install a factory whistle!"

Without turning, Tyler said, "I'm just going to finish this one spot!"

Zoey had no such desire. She cleaned up her work area, then she started on his. Tyler stepped down from his ladder, picked up the remaining tools and supplies, then walked with Zoey to the storage room. They finished packing up then stopped by the office.

Aunt Minnie looked up at Zoey. "I've still got some work to do. Would you mind walking home?"

"Not at all."

Tyler chimed in. "I can give you a lift."

That was thoughtful. "No, thanks. It's not far. I walk it all the time."

Tyler said, "Okay," and the moment passed. They headed for the stage door. Before he even opened the door, Zoey heard pounding rain in the alley.

Aunt Minnie rushed out of her office. "I heard the rain. I'll run you home and come back."

"Don't bother, Minnie," Tyler said. "Your house is on my way home."

Zoey tried to think of an out. But it made the most sense.

Aunt Minnie peered at Tyler, her eyebrows knitted in concern. "Are you sure it's no trouble?"

"No trouble at all." He turned to Zoey. "Shall we?"

"Wait!" Aunt Minnie called. "Take some umbrellas!"

One perk of owning a theater was that patrons often left umbrellas behind. There were always some lying around. So Tyler and Zoey each grabbed one then made a run for Tyler's truck.

As he pulled out onto the road, Zoey said, "It's about a mile down the road."

"I know. I've been there before."

Zoey hadn't expected that. "Really?"

"Oh yeah. Minnie's had me over for dinner." He tossed a knowing expression in Zoey's direction. "That lady can cook."

"Yes, I'm aware."

"Oh, by the way, your high school graduation photo is something."

Zoey grimaced. "She won't take that down. Believe me, I've begged her."

"Why should she? She loves you, and she's very proud of what you've accomplished."

Zoey buried her face in her palm. "And she told you my life's story—the long version, no doubt." She looked up, wincing.

"It's a good story." He glanced over, his expression gentle. "With some sad parts."

"Yeah." Zoey tamped down a wave of unexpected emotion.

He pulled into her driveway and stopped beside the log home. "I'm sorry about your parents—and for bringing it up."

"No, it's okay." She felt oddly relieved. He had broken the ice. It sometimes felt like the elephant in the room that no one wanted to acknowledge. "It's good, actually. I had parents, and they were amazing. Sometimes, people seem uncomfortable if I mention them."

"I could see in the pictures how much they loved you."

Zoey managed a nod.

Tyler's mood suddenly shifted. "I'm starving. Are you hungry?"

She couldn't lie. "Yeah, I guess so."

"Why don't we go get something to eat?"

Zoey froze, mouth open. She closed it. "Well, I was going to, uh, warm up a hot dog and watch the news."

"It's just food."

He's right. It's just food. Not a date. A date would have been planned, and this wasn't.

She nodded. "I like food. Okay."

His eyes sparkled. "Good. Then let's go." He put the truck in gear and headed back onto the road.

FOUR

They opted for the retro chrome diner on the outskirts of town. After choosing a booth in the corner, they glanced at the menus and, having separately been there a number of times, set them down on the edge of the table. Zoey had gone to high school with their server. Those were some memories seared in her brain. Zoey had moved to town as a senior. Everyone else had gone through school together from kindergarten, so their friendships were already formed. Most of her classmates ignored her, but not Shelby Schafer. She'd been relentlessly mean.

Resolving to leave it in the past, Zoey cast one last glance at Shelby, who was now eyeing Tyler. She then caught Zoey's eye and gave her a familiar withering look before disappearing through the swinging doors to the kitchen.

Tyler followed her stare. "Is everything okay?"

Zoey shrugged it off. "Yeah. Fine."

Tyler waited expectantly. "But—"

"It's nothing."

He looked at her evenly.

"Fine. It's our server, Shelby Schafer. I know her from high school. Not one of my best memories."

"Let me guess. Mean?"

"She hated me for some reason. I guess because I was new. When she found out I wasn't going to the prom, she called me a dateless loser. Not exactly clever, but she made her point."

"That must've hurt."

Is this guy for real? No one had ever been so empathetic with her. "It was a long time ago."

He searched her eyes and, with one look, pried the truth from her.

"Okay." *I can't believe I'm telling him this.* She exhaled. "The thing is, I just saw her checking you out like she couldn't believe—" *Too late to stop now.* "Like she couldn't believe I was with you." Zoey looked down, shaking her head.

He leaned forward and nodded. "Because you're way out of my league." He smiled so sincerely it made her heart swell.

Zoey felt her defenses crack. "You are... such a good liar." She grinned broadly.

He leaned back, eyes wide in protest. "I am not! I am telling the truth."

Zoey laughed. "I'm not complaining."

Tyler's expression faltered. "Look, I feel like we got off to a rough start. I'm not trying to push you out of your comfort zone."

All at once, her heart deflated. "My comfort zone? Oh. You've been talking to my aunt."

Tyler seemed at a loss. "I talk to her almost every day."

Now you're just being polite. She thought about him having dinner over there, looking at all her childhood photos while her aunt proudly shared her life story. Of course she had told him. "So she's obviously told you about my..." *Just say it. He already knows.* "Anxiety."

Tyler quietly said, "She might've mentioned you're a little high-strung."

Her old friend Shelby arrived with their food. Zoey wanted to leave, but if she did, Shelby would notice. In a small town like that, it would turn into a story—and she didn't want to hear the version that would come back to her.

"High-strung. That's one way to put it."

"Zoey, it's okay."

"For you, maybe."

"I mean..." He heaved a sigh. "I don't know what it is, but everything I want to say to you seems to come out all wrong."

Zoey pushed her salad around with her fork. "I'm sorry."

Tyler shook his head. "No, that's not what I

mean. It's not your fault. Did you think I was blaming you?"

Zoey gave a half-hearted shrug. "No, but it's me. I push people away. Not always on purpose but sometimes. It's a coping mechanism. Believe it or not, I'm actually doing much better. Therapy and medication work wonders." *Yes, lay it all out there, and then he'll leave you alone. Guaranteed.*

A long silence stretched between them. Zoey finally broke it. "So... you wanted to say something. What was it?"

"Oh, that." What followed was a smile she hadn't seen. He actually looked bashful. "I like you."

She froze for a moment, lost in his gaze. He gave such an honest, gentle look that made her want to believe him. She knew she should say something, but she couldn't form the words.

"I just want to get to know you," Tyler said. "No pressure. Let's just be friends and see how it goes."

At that moment, Zoey's social anxiety dissolved. Somehow, Tyler had managed to tear down a wall that no one else had ever attempted to scale. She looked straight at him and couldn't believe what she was saying. "I'd like that."

They smiled, then Tyler looked down at the food. "We should probably eat this before it gets cold."

In the hour that followed, they talked easily, laughed occasionally, and Zoey, for once, felt entirely at ease. Not only that—she felt happy.

When it came time to leave, Tyler looked around for Shelby to ask for the check. Under his breath, he said, "Zoey, subtly... take a look at your friend."

Zoey followed his eyes to where Shelby stood near the kitchen door with a phone peeking out of her apron pocket. When Zoey turned, she slipped it back out of sight.

The blood drained from Zoe's face. "Was she?"

Tyler nodded.

Shelby had been recording a video of them. Zoey got that nauseous feeling she'd had intermittently throughout her senior year. She stared at the table. "At least this way, I won't hear them laughing about me."

She lifted her eyes to meet Tyler's, but instead of pity, she found anger. "She's a little old for the mean-girl routine."

Zoey's face wrinkled in disbelief. "Have you been on social media? Believe me, no one outgrows it."

"I try to avoid it. I only do what I have to for work." He stared off into the distance thoughtfully. "But I do love movies."

"Yeah, me too." *Hello. My aunt owns a movie theater. Did I miss something?* Zoey clearly wasn't following him.

With a sly smirk, Tyler narrowed his eyes. "Have you done any acting?"

"I took an acting class in college. It seemed like an

interesting way to satisfy that piece of the liberal arts requirement."

Tyler's face broke into a devious grin. As Shelby approached the table, Tyler said, "Just play along."

"I'm not really good at theater improv. I think I failed that unit."

When Shelby arrived at the booth, Tyler looked up. Zoey braced herself, fearing Tyler might say something harsh. That would just make it worse. But instead, he could not have been more pleasant as he asked for the check. He was unbelievably charming. Shelby pulled the check from her apron pocket and handed it to him.

Zoey could see the outline of the phone in the other apron pocket. Surely Tyler didn't intend to take it. That's all they needed—for him to be arrested for assaulting a server. That would fuel the town's gossip mill for days, if not weeks. But he made no such move. He just handed Shelby his credit card and turned back to Zoey.

Zoey tried to give him some money for her half of the meal, but he only shook his head. "Buy me coffee tomorrow, and we'll call it even."

"Okay." She wasn't about to argue with Shelby hovering over them. Besides, she could bring him breakfast in the morning—something delicious from the donut shop in town.

Seeming displeased that Tyler's attention was fixed on Zoey, Shelby turned from the table. When she was well out of earshot, Tyler leaned forward conspiratorially. "What was it she used to call you?"

Zoey frowned. *Do I have to repeat it?* "Dateless loser."

"Let's prove her wrong." His eyes twinkled.

Do I really want to know? "How?"

Before he could answer, Shelby returned and dropped off Tyler's card and receipt. She opened her mouth to say something to Tyler, but a man from another booth cleared his throat and waved Shelby over. Looking reluctant, she left.

Now curious, Zoey asked again, "How?"

"Simple. A stage kiss. Just like in acting class."

"We didn't do any kissing in my acting class."

"It's easy. I'll just put my lips on yours—"

"I know how to kiss! I just—"

"Good. Ready?" Without waiting for an answer, he slipped out of the booth.

Not really! But she followed him, all the while thinking about Shelby and those mean girls—mean women. And those words.

Dateless loser? I'll show you a dateless loser. "I'm ready."

Tyler winked. He hooked an arm about Zoey's shoulders and led her to the door. She liked how his arm felt around her. She began to consider a life in the theater. Behind the counter, Shelby stared at the pair while she wiped the same spot on the laminate surface.

Tyler whispered, "Ready?"

Zoey nodded. *I hope.*

Tyler kissed Zoey's forehead.

Her eyes darted up. *Is that it?*

Then he stopped at the door, took her face in his hands, and put his lips to hers. He kissed her until she felt lightheaded. She wrapped her arms around his neck just in case her knees gave out. Tyler held her against him until she gave in and molded her body to his. Then he ended the kiss and, keeping one arm about her waist, opened the door.

How she made it outside with her wobbly knees she didn't know, but she managed. They walked into the darkness where, she was certain, the stars twinkled brighter than ever before.

With the coast clear, Tyler slipped his arm from her waist and took hold of her hand. "I'm sorry, but I just felt like she had it coming."

Sometimes, you gotta do what you gotta do.

"I just thought, when I saw that camera, why not give her something to record?"

And you did. Can I have a copy? Then she realized she could. Knowing Shelby, that kiss would be on social media within the hour. *Hmmm. My street cred just got an upgrade.*

"You're awfully quiet. Bad idea?" Tyler's eyes were full of concern.

Zoey was still trying to steady her breathing. "No. No, it was perfect." *Just perfect.*

TYLER PULLED INTO THE DRIVEWAY. He wanted to talk. Zoey had been quiet the entire way home. It was a short ride, so maybe he was reading things into it. The lights were on. Minnie's shadow moved about behind the kitchen curtains.

He turned to Zoey. "Thanks for dinner."

"But you bought it."

"I mean for the company."

Zoey smiled, but it looked forced. "You're welcome. Thanks for the food. See you tomorrow."

"Yeah." A long silence followed, then Zoey nodded and opened her door. Tyler escorted her to the porch steps and watched her go safely inside. It was too late to grab her hand, pull her back. Running inside seemed like the wrong thing to do. He laughed inwardly. *And for what? Another kiss?*

Not that he would have minded. But she was gone. He returned to his truck and backed out of the driveway.

On the way home, he couldn't let it go. Something had happened between them—something significant. He felt it. He was pretty sure she did too. Otherwise, things wouldn't have gotten so awkward all of a sudden. It was supposed to have been fun—just a goofball prank on her old bully. When he'd first thought of it, he'd envisioned them bolting to the car then collapsing in their seats, peals of laughter filling his truck.

But then that kiss had happened.

I couldn't be imagining it all, could I? Was it all on my side? From the start, he'd been attracted to her. Anyone would be. After nearly running into him, she'd stared up at him with those big brown eyes, her wavy blond hair framing her face. In one look, he knew she was someone he'd like to know better.

But when they'd started working together at the theater, she'd made it clear that she wasn't interested in him. He'd shifted gears. They would be friends. Friends were good.

Once that was established, the tension between them dissolved—so much so that he felt perfectly comfortable asking her out to eat. It wasn't a date. He thought they had a good time in the diner. She was easy to talk to. The topics were a bit superficial, but they were progressing. Zoey wasn't one to open up easily, but that was okay. Tyler was patient. And judging from the looks of the theater repairs they had ahead of them, they had plenty of time. Things were going so well. *So what happened?*

Tyler had always enjoyed a good practical joke. In that regard, he had never grown up. He'd always felt sorry for people who let themselves grow old and stuffy. As far as he could tell, they did it to themselves. They took the fun out of life just because time had passed. He set no such expectations for himself.

He had seen enough people die to know how precious life was, so he would enjoy his as long as he was able.

The diner kiss was just another practical joke—the prank had served its purpose of getting back at Zoey's high school tormentor. As much as he loved Cedar Creek, Shelby was a reminder that it was a small town, and small-town people gossiped. As he thought about her recording the video for the much larger global platform online, it reminded him how social media brought out the worst in some people.

The look on Zoey's face when she'd described Shelby's nickname for her had been enough to spur Tyler to action. He could still remember the pain in her eyes. She deserved better than cruelty, so he was determined to give it to her.

He'd loved that Zoey had gone all in. He couldn't believe Minnie had described her as high-strung. He saw the spark in her eyes, no doubt reflected from his, as they put their plan into action. They both knew it was fake. The biggest challenge was to keep from laughing until it was over.

But when they'd kissed, nobody laughed.

He imagined what it might be like to be in a relationship with Zoey. It wasn't going to happen. He knew that. But he couldn't help wondering.

His years on the road hadn't been conducive to long-term relationships. Not that he had lived as a monk. There were other women in the same situation

—reporters with a spirit of adventure. People drifted together and, soon after, drifted apart. It was part of the life he had signed up for. But now he was there. Cedar Creek was his home. He had chosen the property, fixed up the cabin, and now he wanted to build the life he had dreamed of.

It seemed he and Zoey were both at a crossroads. He hadn't been able to get much out of her about why she was there. Minnie had mentioned her niece would be moving back home, but she'd said it in passing. Had he known what Zoey would mean to him, he would've paid better attention. Even so, there was something about her, an unsettled aspect that made them seem perfectly suited despite being entirely different. It almost felt as though they were destined to meet.

Oh, right—except for the part where you were barely able to talk her into friendship. Yeah, she's crazy about you! He sighed. They weren't even friends. They were coworkers. Real friends spent time together. Work friends were stuck with each other. *Call it whatever you like, but whatever it is isn't real.*

But that kiss...

Wasn't real.

FIVE

Zoey walked inside and breezed past her aunt.

"Are you hungry?"

"No. Tyler and I grabbed a bite."

"Oh?"

Maybe Zoey was imagining things, but Aunt Minnie sounded a bit too intrigued. It was just food. She paused at her door. "I'm exhausted. I'm going to call it a night."

"Okay, honey."

She could practically hear the wheels turning in her aunt's mind, but to her credit, she had never been one to pry. When she'd first moved into her aunt's, Zoey had been in such a fragile state. At sixteen, she had just lost her parents, and her aunt knew when to tread lightly.

Aunt Minnie had been grieving too. She'd lost a sister. It must have been hard to suddenly deal with a teenaged girl with all Zoey's issues. But three therapists and two psychiatrists later, they'd gotten through it and arrived at a place where the sun shone again.

Zoey hesitated then turned back to her aunt. "Thanks for taking me back."

Aunt Minnie smiled. "It's your home." She made it sound simple.

For Zoey, it was so much more. "Good night, Aunt Minnie."

"Good night, honey."

ZOEY DIDN'T SLEEP WELL. She went through every imaginable interpretation of her evening with Tyler. She had enough going on in her life without him. He was a distraction—an overly good-looking distraction. He had a way of seeing through her eyes and into her heart, and her heart was in no shape to entertain company. But if she had to have someone close, she could almost imagine Tyler being the one. Which was crazy. Absolutely insane. *But what if...?*

Sleep won out before she could answer that question. When her watch beeped, she dragged herself out of bed in time to walk to the theater with a stop on the way.

Tyler's face lit up at the box of donuts and tray of

three coffees. He bounded over to help her with the door.

As he took the tray from her, she said, "I didn't know how you take your coffee."

"Cream, no sugar."

"There's cream and stuff in the bag." Zoey sat down, took a glazed donut for herself, then offered the box to Aunt Minnie.

Aunt Minnie took a coffee and passed on the donuts. Her attention was fixed on her phone. "Zoey?"

"Yeah?"

"Do you remember Shelby Schafer?"

Zoey and Tyler exchanged startled glances.

Aunt Minnie held out her phone.

"May I?" Zoey took the phone from Aunt Minnie and watched the video with Tyler.

Like a skilled film editor, Shelby had cut the table conversation and gone straight to the kiss. She and Tyler watched the whole thing then watched it again.

Aunt Minnie leaned back, coffee in hand. "So, how was dinner?"

AFTER EXPLAINING it all to Aunt Minnie, they had a laugh and went back to work on the plaster. A few hours of hard work later, Tyler and Zoey paused to survey their progress.

Tyler folded his arms. “What do you think, a week?”

“For the lobby and stairs? More or less.”

“Then on to the orchestra and balcony after that?”

“Maybe. Aunt Minnie wants to concentrate on the parts most people see, like the lobby. Oh, that reminds me. It’s Friday. We need to wash the windows and doors.”

They cut the plastering job short to spend the afternoon washing the windows and concession display case, dusting the gift shop shelves, and vacuuming the lobby carpet.

“Has she been managing all this on her own?” Tyler asked when they’d finished.

Zoey shook her head. “She’s got a cleaning crew that comes in on the weekends. They used to come during the week, but she had to cut down their hours.”

Tyler set down the last of the supplies in the storage room. “Has she ever thought about selling?”

Zoey lifted her hand to signal him to be quiet. “Don’t let her hear you say that. Sore subject.”

“Oh, sorry.”

“It’s okay. But the opera house has been in the family for generations. For my aunt, it’s about more than history or sentiment. It’s a family legacy. She would never let it go.”

Tyler paused in the doorway. "I get it. It's just that there's a lot of work here."

"I know. And no money."

"But"—his eyes brightened—"she's got a great work crew!" He combed his fingers through his hair and struck a pose but smeared plaster on a few strands of hair in the process.

"Wait, stop." She pointed to his hair.

"What?"

"Unless you're going prematurely gray, you've just plastered some of your hair."

"What? Where?" He looked around for a mirror.

Zoey shook her head. "Bend down." She ran her fingers through his hair until most of the plaster was gone.

Tyler straightened, then his eyes locked onto hers.

Zoey's heart began to race. Their diner kiss flashed through her mind, and his gravitational pull drew her toward him. She nearly leaned against him but caught herself.

"Got it." She brushed her hands on her pants. "You'll have to get the rest in the shower if there's any left."

He glanced toward the lobby. "Good. Thanks." He walked through the door.

Zoey nodded and followed. "You're welcome. So... lunch."

Tyler hesitated and glanced at his watch.

Thinking he was eager to leave, Zoey blurted, "It's my turn."

He looked surprised.

"To treat you."

Before he could reply, Aunt Minnie walked out of her office with her purse on her shoulder. "I'm off to my book club luncheon." She glanced through the window. "What a beautiful day. And me, stuck indoors." She sighed then brightened. "It's a perfect day for a picnic. Why don't you two take a long lunch? Well, I'm off!" With a cheery wave, she left.

Zoey and Tyler turned from Minnie to each other expectantly.

He hadn't accepted her invite, but he hadn't blown her off either. Finally, she broke the silence. "I guess I could get us some sandwiches."

Tyler's eyes danced. "From the sub shop! Plus, I have the perfect place we can enjoy this weather."

She could practically taste an Italian combo. "Oh, that sounds good!"

Aunt Minnie was right. It was the perfect day for a picnic.

AFTER HEADING out from the sub shop, they drove down a private road then parked in front of a small cabin with a steeply pitched roof and a wrap-around deck.

Tyler made a grand gesture toward the cabin. "This is mine."

"Oh. It's so cute!"

Tyler smirked. "Cute isn't exactly what I was going for."

Zoey bit her lip. "Did I say cute? I meant ruggedly cute."

"Which sounds so much better."

"Doesn't it?"

Zoey surveyed the cabin with its freshly stained logs and metal roof. A fence marked off a neat rectangular yard, which was dotted with newly planted shrubs. "The picket fence is adorable."

Tyler grimaced. "That was here already."

"Oh. Are we having lunch here?"

"No, but if you need to make a pit stop..."

"I'm good." She was curious to see inside, but then she remembered their kiss, and her imagination ran wild. If she took one step inside that place, she might not be able to control herself. She was better off staying outside.

"It's just a short walk." He led her to a mulch-covered trail. "I was wearing a path to this spot, so I decided to make it official and clear it."

A few minutes later, they arrived at a clearing that overlooked a small waterfall. Zoey gasped. "Oh, wow!"

A few feet from the water was a round stone-lined fire pit surrounded by tree stump benches.

Beyond that was a lean-to containing a bed-sized platform.

"I like to camp out, so I built this."

"All this is your land?"

"Don't be too impressed. It's only ten acres."

"It's a gorgeous ten acres."

"I was lucky to find it." He held out his arm toward the fire pit, and they sat on the tree stumps.

While they got settled with their sandwiches and bottles of water, Zoey looked over at him. "Can I ask you a question?"

Tyler grimaced. "Nothing good ever follows that."

Zoey shook her head dismissively. "I was just wondering."

"About?" He took a bite of his sandwich.

"Why the move? Why Cedar Creek?" She looked into his eyes. "I mean, besides your bike outing. What drew you to such a small, unassuming town?"

"The fact that it was such a small, unassuming town. It seemed like a good place to hide from the world."

That piqued Zoe's interest. "There's a story there."

"Yeah. The short version is, I quit my job."

"And the long version?"

"I'm a journalist."

"Oh." That made Cedar Creek seem like an even

further choice for someone like Tyler. He didn't seem the type of reporter to operate out of a storefront, covering local politics, school board meetings, and the occasional charity event.

"I've been a foreign correspondent for the past seven years. My last assignment was Afghanistan."

"Oh my gosh!"

"Yeah." He drew his eyebrows together and set down his sandwich. "It was hard work, but it suited me. At least for a while. It can wear on a person."

"I can imagine."

He stared off into the distance. "You see things you wish you could forget. It's part of the job, but there's this constant balancing act. You have to steel yourself so you can get the job done. But if you let yourself get completely desensitized, you come close to losing your soul."

The same eyes Zoey usually found so expressive were now void of emotion.

"Anyway," he continued, "after things went south and the US pulled out, I left. I had some good contacts who stayed behind—not all voluntarily—so I kept reporting. But my stories weren't getting published. A US drone strike claimed to have stopped a Kabul suicide bomber on the way to the airport. In truth, it struck and killed a family of ten innocent civilians. It took two weeks for the truth of that story to come out."

"I remember the photos of those beautiful children."

Tyler nodded. "And then there were the planes full of citizens and allies that were grounded at Mazar-i-Sharif. Someone above my pay grade sat on that for a week."

"Why?"

"I don't know. You can make yourself crazy with possible theories. What I do know is that the State Department was either stonewalling or ignoring US citizens and Afghans who had helped us for years. They were pleading for help, and no one was listening. They were just left there with years of promises broken. I tried to dig into that story too."

Tyler shook his head. "I was doing my job, but the truth was being buried in talking points and false narratives. People were stranded—they still are—afraid for their lives, and the only people who seemed to care were private citizens. Ex-vets risked their lives to bring people home. Meanwhile, our president hailed a humiliating surrender as an 'extraordinary success.'" Tyler's expression hardened. "It was a disgraceful disaster and a betrayal of good people who'd helped us.

"Even now, to countless Americans and allies abandoned behind enemy lines, our government offers more empty promises that they'll ask the terrorists in charge to release them. It was too much to take, so I quit."

Underneath that toughened exterior, Zoey saw a mix of pain and outrage in his eyes. "I'm sorry you had to go through that."

Tyler shrugged. "I'm lucky. I had the freedom to quit my job and come here."

Zoey wanted to say something encouraging but had no idea what. Perhaps all he needed was for someone to listen.

He turned to her. "Sorry. I didn't mean to unload. This was supposed to be a pleasant picnic lunch."

"I wanted to know. Otherwise, I wouldn't have asked."

"I haven't talked about it to anyone except your aunt. She's a good listener." His lips tilted up in a half smile. "Don't worry. Unlike with you, I just gave her the highlights."

"Aunt Minnie's a great person to talk to. She got me through a tough time."

"You're lucky to have her."

Zoey tamped down a rising wave of emotions. "I am."

"Is that why you moved back?"

"What, for the moral support? I guess, but it wasn't the main reason. I mean, I was doing okay. Aunt Minnie told you about my anxiety."

"Not in so many words, but I figured it out."

Zoey smiled. "That's the ace reporter in you."

Tyler smirked.

Her face fell. "I'm a teacher—was a teacher.

When the lockdowns started, everyone lost their minds, especially the teachers' unions. There I was—the one with the anxiety issues—and I was fine. I did the remote learning, got vaccinated, and basically did what I had to do for my students."

"What grade?"

Zoey's smile returned as she thought of her students, but it was bittersweet. "Third grade. I miss them. I miss the way things used to be."

"I can imagine. So, what happened?"

"Despite teachers' best efforts during the pandemic, our kids basically lost a year of learning. And it's not like they could afford it."

"I did a story once about how US students rank internationally. It's not good."

Zoey nodded. "What students need now is to focus on solid academics to get back up to speed."

Tyler's eyebrows knitted together, but before he could speak, Zoey continued, "I know. It's kind of a 'duh,' right? I mean, there were young students who had forgotten how to read. And basic math skills... well, don't get me started. But instead of addressing the obvious needs, we were told to teach Marxism."

"To third graders?" Tyler's eyes narrowed in disbelief.

"I know. But once you step back and analyze it, it makes sense. If you're looking for big-picture societal change, do a hard sell on the children—our future. I mean, it's been done before with the Hitler Youth."

Tyler looked confused. "But Marxism?"

"I know. It sounds crazy. But next time when you feel like making your head explode, go look up the Frankfurt School. In pre-Nazi Germany, some Marxist guys got together and developed a way to drive social change, which they called critical theory. Fast-forward to a hundred years later. Take critical theory and, like a zany but dangerous word game, cross out every instance of 'class' and substitute 'race.'

Next thing you know, you've got children who've been friends since kindergarten suddenly forming play groups at recess according to whether they're oppressed or oppressors."

"What?"

"I know. It's hard to believe, but if you think about it—and I did—it boils down to basic reverse psychology. Youths don't like being told what to do. So you convince a generation that they're noble rebels effecting positive change. Next, you keep them busy causing chaos so they feel like they're making a difference. In the meantime, you get corporations to donate millions of dollars to organizations that seek to destroy them. Why? Because those young anticapitalists are their biggest customer demographic. It's ironic, I know."

A mischievous smile lit Tyler's face. "It's their way of giving back."

Zoey laughed. "To the corporations? Yeah. It's the circle of life." Her amusement faded. "But it's also despicable to exploit race to advance an unrelated agenda."

Tyler nodded. "Socialism. You know, I just saw a survey in which a quarter of millennials believe individual property ownership is bad for society."

Zoey stared in disbelief. "They should take away their phones and do the survey again."

Tyler laughed. "Oh, the humanity!"

Zoey grew serious. "One day, I looked at the lesson plan, and I couldn't do it. They wanted me to teach this to those innocent children. I couldn't be a part of it."

"So what happened?"

"You know how it works. Either you get with the program or—"

"Quit."

Zoey nodded. "I couldn't sell my soul."

She couldn't bear the sympathy in Tyler's eyes, so she forced a smile to lighten the mood. "So apparently, we have a lot in common. We both have strong principles and no jobs."

Tyler's eyes shone with admiration. "I wouldn't have it any other way. Would you?"

"Well, I do miss the money." She laughed. "But Aunt Minnie understood. She said she was proud of me. She was my safety net. Again."

Tyler's eyes swept over the landscape before them. "Cedar Creek is a good place to reset." He smiled. "The plaster therapy alone is highly curative!"

Zoey nodded. "Ah, yes. That and the dulcet tones of the power drill."

Tyler's expression grew wistful. "I like it. I like helping to bring the old opera house back to its former glory. There's something about that place. All that history just seems to hover in the air."

"Yeah, sometimes you can smell it." She tried not to laugh.

"No, really. It makes me feel like I've gone back in time. Not to mention the layers of paint. You can actually time travel layer by layer."

Zoey shook her head. "What were they thinking in the seventies?"

Tyler lifted his hands helplessly. "Blame it on the psychedelic drugs."

"I guess."

They settled into a companionable silence as they finished their sandwiches. The only sound was the rushing and splashing of water on its way over the falls.

SIX

That night, Zoey sat in bed with her book at her side. Unable to concentrate on reading, she abandoned the effort. Sleep wouldn't come either. She kept reliving the afternoon working with Tyler after their picnic.

They'd continued their usual routine, but the same tasks had somehow felt different with him. There'd been an easiness between them. Tyler had to have felt it. Zoey certainly had.

Her anxiety dropped to a barely noticeable level, although that tended to happen when she was around the same people day after day. But Tyler seemed to regard her in a different light too. She supposed it was natural for them to grow comfortable with each other after spending so much time together. Even so, it felt unique. No matter how many ways she analyzed it, she came to the same conclusion. Her feelings for Tyler were more than mere friendship.

THE NEXT MORNING, Zoey sat in the passenger seat while her aunt drove to the theater.

"So, it's settled," Aunt Minnie said as she pulled onto the main road. "We'll stick with the colors we've got and freshen up the paint in phases. You and Tyler have done an amazing job with the plaster repairs. By the end of today, I think we'll be ready to paint the lobby. We should probably do the restrooms as well. I know it's not exactly where you want to spend a couple days of your life, but it's needed, don't you think?"

Zoey nodded absently. She was too preoccupied with thoughts of Tyler to think about paint.

Unaware of Zoe's inattention, Aunt Minnie continued, "I wish we could go straight through the place, do the house, the balcony—even the backstage area. But that'll have to wait."

"This is a good start at least." It really was. Her aunt had a gift for stretching funds where the theater was concerned.

Aunt Minnie pulled to a stop at a traffic light. "Isn't that Tyler's truck?"

Zoey went into high alert and spotted the truck two cars ahead. "I think so."

The passenger door opened, and a familiar woman got out.

Shelby Schafer?

Shelby walked across the diner parking lot and went in the front door. Zoey froze. Then she felt sick to her stomach.

A car honked behind them, and Aunt Minnie flinched. "Oops!" The light had already changed. With a friendly wave toward the rearview mirror, she drove on.

Aunt Minnie seemed almost as curious as Zoey. "I didn't know he knew her."

"Neither did I." *At least, not in the biblical sense.*

It didn't help that Aunt Minnie grew silent. Zoey could practically hear her mental gears turning. Aunt Minnie had seen the big kiss from Shelby's post. After Zoey and Tyler explained it to her, the three of them had a good laugh, but her aunt was hardly naive.

Zoey desperately tried not to scowl, but Aunt Minnie knew her too well. She had always been able to read Zoey—not that Aunt Minnie was extraordinarily intuitive. Zoey was pitiably poor at concealing her feelings. Her aunt's silence as much as confirmed her likely suspicion that Zoey had feelings for Tyler. It was the only logical explanation for the awkward silence that continued until they arrived at the theater.

Despite having endured the longest one-minute

drive in Cedar Creek history, Zoey set aside all thoughts of her aunt and prepared to face Tyler. She had no intention of confronting him. The last thing she needed was a scene. A new guy, an ugly cry, and a befuddled aunt weren't the best ways to start the day.

Tyler hadn't even done anything wrong. They weren't together. They were friends. Boinking the woman who'd made her senior year in high school a living hell wasn't the most thoughtful thing a friend could do, but it wasn't a crime.

On the other hand, there might be a logical explanation for the cozy drive to work she'd just seen. But she couldn't think of one.

Maybe Tyler thought the kiss in the diner was enough vengeance to teach Shelby a lesson. With justice served, he might've adopted a forgive-and-forget approach. He forgave Shelby and forgot Zoey. She'd just missed when.

Yesterday. After work. Of course. He must have left the theater and gone to the diner to eat. Zoey's scowl deepened. *Then he took Shelby home for dessert.*

Zoey thought for a moment. She was pretty sure she had seen Shelby around town with a boyfriend. *Where was that? Oh well, that's obviously over. And so is my crush on Tyler.* Except it wasn't, and Zoey knew it.

She was reaching for a package of shop rags on the top shelf in the storage room when he walked in.

"Here, let me help you." He stopped close behind her and reached over her shoulder. She smelled soap. He had just showered. She tried not to think about where. Or with whom.

"Thanks." She grabbed it, scooped up some other supplies she had set on the counter, then rushed out of the room.

She didn't stop until she arrived at the last section of lobby wall slated for repair. She couldn't start without Tyler. He had to drill the holes. Only then could she vacuum and apply the adhesive while he circled back and plastered over their prep work. That was the rhythm they'd fallen into, and they'd made considerable progress. Until that moment.

Zoey put on her wireless earbuds and cued up a playlist while she waited for Tyler. When he arrived, he started to say something.

Seeing his lips move, she pulled out one earbud. "Pardon?"

His brow furrowed. "If we work quickly, we might finish by lunch."

"Oh, great." *Got a hot lunch date? Fine.* She just wanted to get the job done and get out. With that to motivate her, Zoey put her earbud back in, cranked up the volume on her phone, and worked with a vengeance.

When it came time for a break, they headed for the coffee machine in Aunt Minnie's office. When Aunt Minnie looked busy, like she did at the moment, they usually walked quietly away, hoping not to disturb her. But that time, Zoey lingered, counting on Tyler to leave without her. She planned to hide out there until break time was over. But Tyler didn't leave.

Aunt Minnie looked up at Zoey from her computer. "Do you need something, honey?"

"I was just thinking..." She spied some paint samples on Aunt Minnie's credenza and walked over to it. "About paint."

Aunt Minnie's eyes twinkled. "Deep thoughts about paint?"

Zoey smiled to cover her embarrassment and tried to ignore Tyler lingering at the back of the office. Paint was the last thing on her mind, and she was sure Aunt Minnie knew it.

"We'll probably finish patching the plaster in the lobby this morning. As soon as it dries, we'll be ready to paint."

Aunt Minnie looked like she was trying to be patient.

"So, uh... what color scheme are we going with?"

Aunt Minnie eyed her suspiciously. "Didn't we talk about this? I guess not. Well, it's a big job, so I've decided to tackle it in stages. If we stick to the original colors, we can phase in the improvements—hopefully without making the whole place look like a crazy quilt. I also just like the idea of keeping the original colors to preserve the historical authenticity."

Zoey shuffled a stack of paint swatches. "That makes sense."

"Well, the truth is, I don't have a choice. There isn't enough in the theater account to finance the whole thing at once, so I have to wait for the funds to come in before I can send them back out again."

Tyler pushed away from the wall he'd been leaning on and peered at Zoey. "Ready?"

AS TYLER APPROACHED the last unfinished section of wall, he glanced at Zoey. She already had her phone out, earbuds in and paired, and was choosing a playlist. It wasn't that unusual. Music was a great way to pass the time while doing a tedious task. It was just that Zoey had never listened to music while working with him. They'd always talked to each other—so much so that, in their short time together, they'd covered a lot of ground. Tyler felt like he knew her, and if that was true, something was bothering her.

Two hours passed during which they exchanged no more than a handful of words. Then Tyler pulled out three pints of paint color samples. He painted an unplastered section of the wall with the different shades and studied them.

"It'll change as it dries, but I think the second shade might be the one." He turned to Zoey, but she didn't respond. He waved his hands in front of her and pointed to his ears.

Zoey pulled out her earbuds.

"I said, they'll change as they dry, but so far, which one do you think looks closest?"

"The second." She started to put her earbuds back in, but she lost her grip. "No!"

The earbud flew from her hand and landed in the paint can.

"No." She stared helplessly as it sank into the liquid.

Seconds passed while Tyler tried to think of the right thing to say. *It'll dry? That color will complement your amber earwax? That's a great color for listening to the blues?*

But before he could say a word, Zoey suddenly excused herself and rushed out through the stage door.

Tyler watched. *I should follow. That's the right thing to do.* He heaved a sigh and made his way after her, wondering if there was a full moon. He could think of no other explanation for the weird day it had turned out to be.

When he opened the door, he found Zoey sitting on the cement steps outside. She was turning the remaining earbud over and over.

Tyler sat down beside her. "Sorry about the earbud. I feel responsible."

She frowned. "Why?"

"If I hadn't spoken to you—"

"It's okay. I'm just... never mind."

Tyler hesitated. Even before the unfortunate earbud incident, she'd been distant all morning. Something was wrong, and he had a feeling it had something to do with him.

He braced himself. "Zoey, what is it?"

She smirked. "An earbud."

He rolled his eyes. "You know that's not what I mean."

She stared ahead silently.

When he couldn't take anymore, he snapped. "What did I do?" After he said it, he realized he might have sounded a little too frustrated.

She cast a wounded glance at him. "Nothing."

He heaved a sigh. "I'm no good at drama. Just tell me."

Zoey looked pained. "I'm not trying to be dramatic."

"Sorry. That came out wrong."

"This morning, Aunt Minnie and I were a few cars behind you." She hesitated then found her voice again. "And we saw you—"

It didn't take him long to figure out what she meant. "With Shelby?" Tyler tried not to smile. "You're not jealous, are you?"

"No! What's the matter with you? This isn't middle school."

"No, it isn't." *But it feels a lot like it.* He didn't want to argue. She could believe him or not. The whole thing made him want to walk away, but he drew in a breath and exhaled.

She frowned. "The thing is, I thought we were friends."

"I think we are friends." Tyler proceeded with caution. "Are you saying I betrayed that by giving Shelby a ride?"

"Is that what they're calling it nowadays?"

Tyler leveled an annoyed look at her. "Yes." Until now, he had been fairly calm, but she was testing his patience. "I gave her a ride in my truck."

"That's okay. I don't need the details."

"Oh? I think you do." He took a moment to calm himself. "Whatever sordid liaison you're imagining never happened."

She didn't reply. She didn't have to. Her disapproval filled the air. Heck, it practically displaced the oxygen.

"Not that you deserve an explanation, but this morning, I was driving to work. As you know, the main road that runs through town is not exactly pedestrian friendly. I saw your friend Shelby walking, so I pulled over and asked if she needed a lift. Her face was red and puffy, like she'd been crying. I didn't ask. I offered her a napkin, and when we hit the red light by the diner, she thanked me and hopped out of the truck. End of story."

Zoey stared at her lone earbud and frowned. "So... you were just being nice?"

He scoffed. "Yeah."

She shook her head. "I thought—"

"Oh, I know what you thought."

Zoey's eyes flitted toward him.

"But just for the record, I'm allowed to have a social life."

Zoey looked offended. "I never said that you weren't. I told you I wasn't jealous." She practically sneered.

"Got it." Tyler didn't even try to suppress the grin that followed.

Zoey let out an indignant laugh. "Oh my gosh! Don't flatter yourself."

"Why not? Somebody's got to, and it's obviously not going to be you."

"What's that supposed to mean?"

"I think we're done here." He got to his feet and turned back to the stage door. "Now we're just bickering."

"We are not!"

Tyler managed a smile, but he was sure his exasperation showed through. There was nothing more to say. Or if there was, he was too weary to say it.

SEVEN

The plaster needed to dry overnight, so they were done for the day. With the afternoon off, Zoey told her aunt she felt like walking home. That gave her a good half hour to agonize over Tyler.

He'd been right. She had been jealous. She claimed to not want a relationship, then she'd acted like they had one. But even if they did, she would've ruined it by acting petty. *I should never have let myself get to this point.*

She had been through a similar pattern before. According to her therapist, it had to do with losing her parents. She had some sort of underlying instinct to protect herself from letting others in. If she kept her distance, it wouldn't hurt as much if she lost them. The thing was, despite her therapist's suggestion that it might not be healthy, it had served her well enough. Until Tyler.

Her heart had gotten the better of her logic. Then her anxiety, which was always at the ready, stepped in to make a mess of it all.

Zoey heaved a sigh. Tyler must have realized she liked him. Her jealousy had totally exposed her. She wanted more than friendship but couldn't seem to let herself have it. Not that he would have anything more to do with her after the Shelby fiasco. *Problem solved. No more Tyler.*

It's for the best. Or it would be. Eventually. When her heart stopped taking flight every time she looked into his eyes, she would be glad it was all in the past.

It was dusk when Aunt Minnie arrived home. Zoey emerged from her room to touch base.

Aunt Minnie set two bags on the counter. As the two of them unpacked the groceries, her aunt said, "You'll never guess what happened after you left."

After spending a miserable afternoon trying to forget about Tyler, Zoey wasn't in the mood for guessing games, so she waited.

"One of our faithful theater patrons popped in unannounced. Walt Whitmer."

"Isn't that a poet?"

"Walt Whitman. I'll bet he gets that a lot. Anyway, he's one of our regular volunteers." A spark lit up her eyes. "I think he might have a soft spot for me."

Zoey offered her aunt a polite smile.

"So, he looks around and asks what's going on

with all the fresh plaster. Then he tells me he used to be a painter—houses, not art. He said he's still got his equipment, then he offers to paint the whole lobby."

"Oh, wow."

"He's got one of those power spray things, so he said it would go pretty fast." Aunt Minnie shrugged. "So he's going to paint, and you've got the week off."

"But won't Walt need some help?"

She shook her head. "He said he works solo. So I'm making him lunch and, if he plays his cards right, maybe dinner." She grinned.

Zoey loved her aunt, but the thought of her canoodling with Walt—or anyone, really—made her queasy. "Okay. Well, that gives me a week to take care of some things I've been putting off. Like looking for a job."

Aunt Minnie looked sympathetic. "As soon as business picks up at the theater, I can pay you for what you do around there."

Zoey held up her hand in protest. "Free rent's a pretty good deal."

Aunt Minnie huffed. "Rent? Don't be silly. This is your home." She gave Zoey a loving smile. "We're family. We're helping each other. That's what families do."

Zoey blinked away a tear then helped her aunt prepare dinner.

HER WEEK OFF was nearly over. She hadn't landed an interview, let alone a job. Cedar Creek was not only a small town but a remote one. The teachers were lifers, and most of the businesses were small family-run operations with a reliable workforce made up mostly of family and close friends. Telecommuting might be a great option, but nothing had panned out on that front.

She set her laptop on the kitchen table and clicked her favorite job-hunting bookmark but decided to make coffee instead. The coffee grinder had barely stopped when the doorbell rang. Zoey looked at her watch. It was about time for one of Aunt Minnie's online shopping deliveries. She went to the front door and looked through the peephole. *Tyler?*

Zoey wished she hadn't spent her time off pining over Tyler, but she had. She just wanted to get over him. *It would help if you'd leave me alone so I can stop liking you.* But deep down, she was happy to see him. She opened the door.

He looked serious. "Hi."

"Hi."

"Can we talk?"

She should have mustered a "no," but instead, she stepped aside and gestured for him to come in. "Sure. Want some coffee? I was just making a pot." That bought her time to regain her composure.

"Okay." He sat down at the kitchen table.

When she was finished, she set down his mug and a carton of half-and-half. "Cream, no sugar?"

Tyler flashed that smile that always gave her butterflies. "You remembered." He poured it into his coffee and handed back the carton.

Zoey joined him, and they both took a drink from their mugs.

With no warning, he set a small box on the table and slid it toward her.

"What's this?"

"Earbuds."

"But—" At a loss for words, she shook her head slowly.

"It was kind of my fault, so there you go. Good as new—because they are new."

"They're more expensive than the ones I lost."

Tyler shrugged. "Yeah, well, I thought about keeping one for myself since, technically, I just caused you to lose one. But I was in a generous mood." His eyes sparkled.

"Tyler, that was so... nice." Her voice caught in her throat. She was genuinely moved.

He looked at her strangely. "They're just earbuds."

Embarrassed, Zoey looked down. "I know, but outside of my family, no one's ever given me 'just earbuds.'" *Or anything else, for that matter.*

He peered at her as though she were some sort of fascinating newly discovered specimen. "I'm sorry."

"Sorry for what? You just did something really nice. Thank you."

"You're welcome." He took another sip of coffee then set down the mug. With a nod toward her laptop, he said, "I can see I caught you in the middle of something, so I'll let you get on with your day."

Zoey wanted to protest and invite him to stay, but she couldn't find the right words. She felt awkward. She had since he'd first shown up at the door. After a week of doing her best to convince herself that any feelings she had for Tyler weren't romantic, he'd walked in and destroyed all her progress.

She rose and walked him to the door. Once there, he paused and turned to face her. "I missed you." He gazed deeply into her eyes.

That was all it took to pierce her emotional force field. "I missed you too."

"Good." With a satisfied smile, he turned and left.

Good? And what's that supposed to mean? But the anxiety spinning her thoughts lost out to the words her heart had needed to hear. *He missed me.* The thought filled her with uncontrollable joy. *He missed me!*

THE FOLLOWING MONDAY, Zoey returned to the theater and was delighted by the sight of the fresh paint. Her heart raced when Tyler arrived, and he joined her in admiring the finished product.

She scanned the walls. "You can't even see where we plastered."

"That's how it should be."

Aunt Minnie emerged from her office. "I thought I heard voices. So, what do you think?"

"It looks great," Tyler said.

"Look what we did!" Zoey couldn't stop smiling, although that wasn't solely because of the paint job.

Tyler turned to Aunt Minnie. "What's next?"

Aunt Minnie winked. "You are a glutton for punishment, aren't you?"

Tyler shook his head. "One of my goals when I moved here was to contribute to the community. It's my new home. Besides, work is therapeutic for me."

Aunt Minnie patted his shoulder. "You have a gift for making me feel like I'm doing you a favor."

"You are!" He grinned.

"Then what I'm about to say is going to disappoint you. I've reached a stopping point." She paused as if deciding whether to go on. "Moneywise. In a month or so, we should have enough income in the theater account to proceed. But for now, we're on a hiatus."

Tyler nodded. Having looked at the books, Zoey wasn't surprised.

Aunt Minnie took in a deep breath and exhaled.

With a smile, she said, "So why don't you two go do something fun for a change?"

Zoey got the distinct impression that her aunt meant together. She liked the idea, but then the anxiety gripped her. She looked anywhere but at Tyler.

Aunt Minnie glanced at her watch. "Well, I better go. I have a Zoom meeting with my broker." With that, her aunt turned and went back to her office.

Her broker? Zoey mumbled, "I didn't know she had a broker." She hadn't meant to say that out loud.

"It makes sense, though," Tyler said. "A woman her age—old enough to retire—is bound to have stashed a little nest egg away over the years."

"I guess." She stared blankly at her aunt's office door.

Tyler let out an exaggerated sigh. "I'd really hate to disappoint your aunt."

"Then don't." *What is he talking about?*

He acted relieved, but there was something about the look in his eyes that made Zoey suspect he was up to something. Then he proved it. "So we're both on the same page."

"Are we?"

"Yes. We're going to do something fun."

"We are?"

Tyler lifted his palms. "Well, yeah. For Aunt

Minnie." He grinned. "Having fun doesn't sound so bad, does it?"

"I guess not, but—"

"Good. I'll drive."

"Works for me. I don't have a car."

Before she had time to comprehend what he was doing, he took her hand and headed for the door.

"Wait. Where are we going?"

Tyler kept walking. "It's too early for lunch. And we've already done the picnic thing. We wouldn't want to get into a rut."

She blinked. "No, I guess not."

He pulled out of the parking lot, drove down the road a half mile, then pulled into the bagel shop. "Be right back. Don't drive away without me."

"Okay."

He returned a few minutes later with a bag and two coffees. As he hopped into the truck, he said, "Okay, maybe we are in a rut, but I like food. Besides, this is breakfast—totally different from a lunch picnic."

"As long as there's coffee, I have no complaints."

"Good." He put his hand on hers for a moment.

It was barely a touch, but it felt like so much more to Zoey. She liked it. No, she loved it. And yet she wasn't prepared for the surge of overwhelming emotions. It wasn't Tyler's fault. He'd done nothing wrong. The poor guy had no clue that she was a walking bundle of anxiety. She had never gotten so close to anyone in a relationship. She'd had a couple of flings in college, but those had been different. Those guys had been attractive, but she had never felt especially invested emotionally. They'd been more of a chemical thing. It was when her heart got involved that her anxiety grabbed hold and took over. It was to Tyler's credit that they'd made it so far together.

He parked the truck. "Here we are."

"Where?" She looked up to see they'd stopped at the base of a slope. She'd been so consumed by her thoughts that it hadn't even registered that they'd been driving uphill.

"I'm sure it must have a name, but I don't know what it is. We might even be trespassing. So if anyone comes out with a shotgun, run for the truck."

"What? Let's just go."

Tyler laughed. "I'm kidding. A guy in the bagel shop told me about this."

"Some random guy in the bagel shop told you to drive up here?"

Tyler's eyes shone when he smiled, so much so that Zoey barely cared if he gave her an answer. "Well, I asked where I could find the best view around here. When I explained you were with me—"

"Me?"

"Well, I said there was a pretty woman involved."

Pretty?

"And he said to try here. He owns that farm over

there." Tyler grabbed the bag and his coffee then hopped out of the truck. He surveyed the landscape. "There it is."

"There what is?"

Tyler's eyes twinkled. "Our destiny?" Before she could ask him to explain, he winked. "Or a path. He said it was next to a gnarled apple tree. And there it is."

They hiked about a quarter of a mile up to a tree stump that seemed to have been placed there for sitting and taking advantage of the spectacular view. Below, Cedar Creek sparkled in the daylight as the sun wound its way through the hills.

Zoey inhaled sharply. "Oh, wow!"

"Yeah. Remind me to frequent that bagel place more."

They sat down on the stump, and Tyler handed her a bagel.

Zoey took a sip of coffee as she took in the view. "It's perfect," she whispered.

"Your coffee?" His mouth twitched at the corners.

"This moment. The view."

"I'm glad."

Tyler was staring at her. She could feel the full weight of his eyes on her, but she kept her eyes straight ahead.

From the corner of her eye, she saw his head turn

to look back toward the valley. "I've been wanting to talk to you."

The butterflies started. That fluttering feeling would turn to churning uneasiness. She did her four-count breathing.

"I hoped bringing you someplace spectacular might help my cause."

His cause? She couldn't help herself. She faced him. His expression was so vulnerable that she nearly forgot her anxiety and instead felt the need to reassure him. "Why would you need to do that?"

"Because I'm lost. I don't know where I stand with you." He gazed into her eyes. "But I want to."

Zoey's heart swelled. Then the familiar fear gripped her. But she had a gut feeling that it was her chance. If she didn't face up to her feelings, she might never get another. She wasn't even sure what to say, but she just hoped it would come out the right way.

Zoey inhaled slowly. "We might not have painted a clear enough picture, Aunt Minnie and I. I'm not high-strung. It's clinical—as in therapist, psychiatrist, and three medications. Even then, I'm not always quite right. Usually, I'm okay."

Zoey looked out at the beautiful view, barely taking it in. She stole a quick look at Tyler. He was listening. He didn't look horrified yet. That was a good sign. "I've never had a meaningful, long-term relationship. When things get close, I get overwhelmed... and I panic." She glanced at him. "Like right now."

Tyler nodded as though he understood, which was impossible. She didn't understand it herself. But she couldn't stop there. "There've been a few times I thought things might work out, but I couldn't."

"Couldn't what?"

She felt the tears coming. *Not now.* "I couldn't open up. My feelings just sort of shut down."

"Did you explain this to any of them?"

"No!" That came out too emphatically, so she tried to calm down. "I've never told anyone. Until now." She forced herself to look at him. "Until you."

He smiled with a warmth that would have calmed anyone else.

Having come this far, Zoey was determined to finish. "So, to answer your question—well, I guess it wasn't really a question, but that's where you stand with me." She exhaled, waiting for the rejection that would shatter her. But it never came.

"Let's just take our time, then. Okay?"

Zoey was too overwhelmed to speak, so she nodded.

Tyler put his arm around her shoulders and drew her close while they took in the view.

EIGHT

Zoey was all he could think of the entire drive home. She was changing his whole outlook on life. Wherever he looked, he saw choices he wasn't ready to make. He had just left his job for a complete career shift. He'd bought a new home and rebuilt it. He was settling into a new community. His world had already turned on its head. And then there was Zoey. His life started skewing toward her.

The cabin had always been a dream. For years, he had saved, hoping to buy his own personal respite from work. The plan was to someday make it a permanent home. But without the direction or the stability of a job, he was left questioning what to do with his life. He'd already been restless when the idea struck him to help Minnie. He had the time. Staying busy gave him the chance to focus on someone else while he sorted his problems out.

Then he'd met Zoey. The more he got to know her, the more his world seemed to tilt, and he couldn't quite get his footing. It wasn't her fault. She couldn't know how she'd sent him reeling. He might have managed better if he hadn't already left his job and moved to a new place. But there were no constants left in his life anymore. Everything seemed to be floating, weightless, himself included. He kept trying to grasp hold of something, but he couldn't quite reach.

Tyler parked the truck, went inside, and lit a fire to take the edge off of the evening chill. He sank into his leather armchair by the fireplace and put his feet on the ottoman.

Today had been a tremendous breakthrough. He hadn't understood what Zoey struggled with every day. Although he might never fully understand her, he'd made progress today. She had trusted him enough to share something deeply personal. For the first time since they'd met, he thought he might have a chance.

What Zoey needed was time, something he'd never had to bother with where women were concerned. His career had taken him to dangerous places. The people he'd worked with and the women he socialized with were well aware that each day could be their last. So they lived life with a sense of urgency, seizing as much as they could in the time that they had. No one thought about the future. They lived in the moment. It was all about taking. Whether it was solace or comfort or simply someone to cling to in the darkness, they took it.

His feelings for Zoey were all about giving. Maybe that was how he knew it was love. Somehow, as much as he wanted to hold her and kiss her, he had to take his cues from her. What he had with Zoey may have begun with a friendship, but he knew it would grow. It would blossom at its own pace—a pace Zoey could handle. She deserved that.

Perhaps he needed the time as much as she did. His reason for moving to Cedar Creek was to make time to recover from career burnout. But a few weeks had passed, and the pressure had returned. This time, it was self-imposed. When faced with a challenge, his natural tendency had always been to dig in and make it happen, whatever it took. But forcing things with Zoey would only make matters worse. If he'd broken his leg, it would take time to heal. The only miracle cure for him would be to let himself heal naturally.

Everything that mattered lately revolved around time. It reminded him of the huge clock in the Musee D'Orsay in Paris. The first time he'd seen it, he was wandering alone through the museum. With a parting cloud, it suddenly appeared, backlit by the sunlight. He stood there for a long while, gazing through the enormous clock face at the Seine as it flowed through the city. Only time had stood between him and the city of Paris.

It will all work out. Be patient. At least, that was what he kept telling himself. The conversation on the ridge had shown progress, but Zoey had so much further to go before she would open her heart to him. And that was the challenge. From that point on, he would have to hold back the true depth of his feelings until she was ready.

He leaned back in his chair and stared at the ceiling. He didn't know when it had happened, but it was the first time he'd been able to put it into words. He was falling in love.

By then, most of his friends were married. Many had children. He'd watched them go through all of the typical life-changing moments, but he took it for granted because that was what people did. Years ago, when the first of his friends had fallen in love, Tyler had asked them how they knew it was love. He'd repeated the question over several years with different friends. They'd all shared different versions of the same thing, and it had never made sense. Until Zoey. It must have been happening from the moment he'd met her, and their answers flooded his mind. He just knew. That was how every one of them described it to him.

He wasn't sure how, wishful thinking perhaps, but he sensed that she loved him already. Her love seemed to be entangled in crippling emotions, but he was determined to help Zoey break through them. Determined but clueless as to how.

HIS PHONE RANG. He felt a twinge of disappointment when it wasn't Zoey. *Sean Murphy?*

"Hey, Murph. What's up?"

"Farrington! How are you?"

"I'm good. I'm sitting in my mountain cabin."

"You're kidding! So you finally did it? Wait—don't tell me. You're in a leather chair with your feet up on a leather ottoman, and there's a fire in the fireplace and a whiskey in your hand."

"Close. I had to set down my glass to answer the phone."

Murph laughed. "So, where are you?"

"The Adirondacks. I live outside a little town nobody's heard of. Good people. Good living."

"It's about time you did it. You've only been talking about it since I've known you."

Tyler grinned. "How 'bout you? Still married with thirteen kids?"

"Five."

"Wow. Look at us. Could we be any more predictable?"

Murph chuckled. "Actually, I've got something that might surprise you."

"Yeah? Well, good, because usually you're just so damn boring."

"Hey, watch it, or I might not tell you about the job I'm about to offer you."

"A job? Here in Cedar Creek?" Tyler chuckled to himself.

"No, actually, I got a promotion. Hard to believe, but I'm a senior editor now, and we need someone to pick up some freelance work now and then. You were the first person I thought of."

Tyler put his feet on the floor and sat at the edge of his chair. "Yes."

"Yes?"

"Yeah!"

Although he had enough money to last for six months to a year, depending on how comfortably he lived, he didn't want to burn through his savings. Especially if he was going to build something with Zoey. He didn't know where it was going, but he didn't want money—or lack of it—to get in the way. Freelancing might just fit the bill. He could work when he wanted. He wouldn't have to be away all the time. Most of all, the separation might be good for Zoey. A brief break now and then would give her a breather and, he hoped, ease her anxiety.

"Let me tell you the details first before you officially agree." Murphy launched right into the money. There weren't any benefits for freelancers. That came as no surprise. But the money wasn't bad. "Right now—and I mean right now—we need someone to go down to Texas to cover the border."

"Okay."

"Really? I mean, like, tomorrow."

They worked out the best airports to get him there. Albany was at the top of the list, but Syracuse could work too. Murphy said he would get the details to Tyler later that night and have him on a plane bound for Texas first thing in the morning.

Tyler hung up the phone and stared into the fire. Freelancing might give him the control that he sought over his work or, at least, control over the projects he took on. They hadn't talked about the length of the assignments. He didn't want to go back to spending months at a time in third-world countries and war zones. But for the moment, he would do the border job and take things from there.

ZOEY WAS CURLED up on her comforter with yet another book she'd given up reading when her phone rang. Tyler was going away. He wasn't sure, but he didn't think he would be gone for more than a week.

"I'll call you when I get back," he said.

"Okay."

He hesitated but then said, "Bye, Zoey."

"Bye. Have a good trip." She cringed. *Have a good trip? He's going to the southern border of Texas, where it's 105 degrees. How good could anything be at that temperature?*

They hung up without her saying the words she'd wanted to. *I'll miss you.*

IN THE WEEK THAT FOLLOWED, Zoey filled the time by cooking up a storm. She delved deeply into internet recipes and menu apps and cleaned Aunt Minnie's house twice. She'd read somewhere that housework counted as exercise, so she felt doubly accomplished. When thoughts of Tyler tortured her, she put in her earbuds—the ones he had given her—and cranked up the music.

But she missed him.

He texted daily. Zoey had told him she couldn't do video calls. They made her uneasy. But their text messages seemed cold and stilted. While Zoey appreciated the news, she could get that from TV or the internet. But after five days, all her frustration vanished the instant her phone rang.

"Zoey?" He barely got out his name before she interrupted him.

"Tyler, how are you?"

"I'm good. How are you?"

"Good." *I miss you. Just say it. I miss you.* But she couldn't.

"I was hoping to be home in a couple of days, but they've asked me to stay on for another week."

"Oh."

A long pause followed, then Tyler said what she couldn't. "I miss you."

Zoey thought her heart might explode. "I miss you too." She covered the phone and exhaled. *I said it! And he said it!*

He talked about how hot it was, what he was writing about, and when it would be published. She was still so overcome that she replied on autopilot. She couldn't remember any of it because all that mattered was that he missed her. She couldn't believe she had told him the same. It had popped out, and at that moment, she felt like dancing—or running a marathon. She hated running, but for Tyler, she would make an exception.

"I wish you were here," he said. "Any chance you might hop on a plane? My treat."

Zoey fell from the heights she'd just soared to, and her landing was hard. "Tyler... that's not a good idea."

"That's okay. I know travel isn't your thing. Just thought I'd throw it out there."

"Thanks. I-I've got to go. It was good to talk to you."

Zoey curled up on her bed with her phone in her hand. If only she could.

TYLER STARED AT HIS PHONE. *Tyler Farrington, you are an idiot.* All of his plans to go slowly just went up in smoke with one question. He'd pushed her too far. He'd heard it in her voice just before she'd hung up.

They texted back and forth a few times in the following days, but it wasn't the same, and he knew it wouldn't be until he could see her again. He poured himself into his work, which was not all that difficult. There was a lot going on.

AUNT MINNIE WALKED through the door. "What is this?"

"Chicken pot pie. I'm trying to improve my pie crust skill. It's not as flaky as I'd like, but I think I'm getting better."

Her aunt looked at the pie. "That, my dear, looks gorgeous."

A smile bloomed on Zoey's face. "Really?"

"Yes, really."

The doorbell rang.

Zoey looked up. "Another delivery?"

Aunt Minnie looked clueless. "I don't think so. Unless I've forgotten, which is entirely possible." She pulled out her phone and looked up her most recent orders.

Zoey opened the door. "Tyler." She started to smile, but her face seemed to freeze on the way.

"Tyler?" Aunt Minnie went to the door and stood behind Zoey. "Come in!"

Before Zoey knew what was happening, her aunt had invited Tyler over for dinner. She talked up Zoey's pot pie so much that Zoey feared only disappointment could follow. But they sat down and ate.

Aunt Minnie kept the conversation going while Zoey tried to look calm, but she was so happy to see Tyler that it practically paralyzed her. She interjected a monosyllabic response now and then. Despite her emotional issues, she loved hearing Tyler share stories about his trip. She loved the sound of his voice. Loved being with him. She wondered if she didn't just love him.

When they finished eating, Aunt Minnie apologized and excused herself to watch her favorite TV show. Zoey was sure her aunt was just trying to give her and Tyler privacy. Not that she minded. She'd almost calmed down enough to look normal.

Tyler helped clear the table and load the dishwasher. As Zoey hung the dish towel over the oven door handle, Tyler turned to her.

"There's almost a full moon tonight, and the sky's full of stars. Let's go for a walk."

"Okay." *Two syllables. That's progress.* She pulled on her fleece jacket, and Tyler held the door open for her. Once outside, he took Zoey's hand. It felt natural walking along, holding hands. She could get used to that.

Tyler was right. In the midst of a pitch-black blanket that glittered with stars, the moon cast a silver glow over the land.

Tyler squeezed Zoey's hand. "I missed you."

"Me too."

He stopped and turned to face her. "Would a hug be okay?" He stretched out his arms, and when she stepped toward him, he drew her into an embrace.

He was solid and warm. She took in a deep breath. His scent was familiar and comforting. Being in his arms was like coming home.

He released her and reached into his pocket. "I brought you back something."

She opened her mouth in surprise, but no words came to mind. It didn't matter what it was. She was touched by the gesture alone.

He took her hand and stretched an elastic bracelet over it. She held it up to the moonlight for a closer look.

"It's hand-painted," Tyler explained. "Those are bluebonnets, the state flower."

"It's pretty. Thank you!" She wanted to give him a hug but hesitated. *Why do I have to be like this?* Couples hugged, and they made it look easy. She hoped he was patient enough to wait until they reached that point.

"It's just a little something, but I wanted you to know I was thinking of you."

"Thank you." She would have told him how much she'd been thinking of him too. She thought about him every day, every hour, and almost every minute. But she couldn't imagine herself saying all that without sounding weird or needy. So she said nothing.

Tyler smiled and turned to continue their walk. He took her hand again, and they strolled under the stars in silence. With no pressure to talk, she felt comfortable. It might not last, but for a few minutes, her anxiety and uncertainty settled into a comfortable place. Everything was all right for now. Time would sort out the rest.

A cool breeze brushed past them. Zoey shivered.

"Are you cold? Let's get you back inside."

She was cold, but she didn't want the feeling of being next to him to end. When Tyler put his arm around her shoulders and held her close, she believed that, just maybe, it wouldn't have to.

NINE

Zoey was just waking up when her phone dinged with an incoming text. She brushed her hair out of her eyes and put on her glasses. She smiled to see it was from Tyler.

Are you busy today?

Let me check my calendar. Haha. No.

Her phone dinged again. *Pick one: zip-lining, rock climbing, or white-water rafting.*

By the time she finished reading, her smile was gone. Zoey blinked. None of the above, her first choice, hadn't been an option. She reread the message then typed, *No! No!! And... I guess.*

After all, she knew Cedar Creek pretty well. The rapids couldn't be that bad.

Zoey wasn't sure what one wore to go rafting. It was too early in the season for bathing suits, so she opted for yoga pants, a long-sleeved shirt, and a waterproof softshell jacket. She wasn't sure what else Tyler might have planned, so she shoved a change of clothes in her backpack just in case.

Tyler picked her up promptly. He looked awfully enthusiastic for seven in the morning.

As he drove, Tyler told her their itinerary. "I've only booked half a day. I figured the full-day trip could wait for the next time."

Zoey frowned. *Full day? Next time?* She thought she was being pretty cooperative. It was one of those things people did early on in a relationship before they felt secure enough to say, "No, I don't do life-threatening activities—no matter how hot you look in your cool outdoor gear." And he did look hot. Really hot.

That was the paradox that had always plagued her. She'd always been drawn to athletic guys, with their square jaws and muscular physiques. Which was all fine unless he wanted to do athletic activities as a couple. But the guys who spent sunny days in dimly lit museums and libraries didn't have sun-tarnished faces or well-defined shoulders or biceps that strained the seams of their T-shirts.

Which brought Zoey to her present circumstance. She wanted to spend a half day with Tyler. Heck, she would even spend the whole day with him. Just not in an outdoorsy setting.

Tyler pulled into the parking lot. "Ready?"

"Wait, that says Hudson River. I thought we were going to raft down Cedar Creek."

He looked patiently at her. "I don't think Cedar Creek has white water. It's just got the regular kind."

"I like regular water."

"But white water's more fun." His jaw dropped, but he quickly recovered. "I didn't think to ask if you know how to swim."

"I do. I used to do laps at our health club in the city."

He looked relieved, but his eyes hinted at lingering concern. "The thing is, I thought it might be fun to step just a little outside of our comfort zones."

"I don't know about your comfort zone, but I left mine a few miles back."

He thought for a moment. "We should go home. We could go get some breakfast and find something to do. I screwed up. I was hoping... I thought this might... be good for us."

For me. Zoey watched the other people arriving and going to check in. They were laughing. Everyone was having such fun, and they hadn't even started rafting. She envied them. She would always be on the outside looking in unless she tried to meet Tyler halfway.

What am I afraid of? She was a strong swimmer. Of course, that had been in a pool with calm water. But she did know some basic lifesaving techniques. She had taken a class. She hadn't finished it, but other than that, there was no reason she couldn't sit in a raft.

Tyler put the key in the ignition, and Zoey surprised herself when she put her hand on his. "Come on. Let's go white-water rafting."

"No, you don't have to do this."

She lifted her chin. "I know. Come on. Let's go."

"Are you sure?"

"Yes. Absolutely." She almost believed herself.

Minutes later, they checked in and suited up in helmets and life jackets. They took a bus ride to the launching point, then they gathered around their guide with a handful of fellow rafters for a brief orientation. Their guide was extremely informative as he shared thorough safety instructions. Zoey hadn't actually thought of how many things could go wrong. A lot, apparently. Falling out of the raft was *normal*. Expected, even.

Their guide finished with a less-than-encouraging "We've got the best safety record in the state."

But what if they're all terrible? Zoey turned to more positive thoughts. She envisioned the Hudson River on the west side of Manhattan. It had seemed calm enough there. *How bad can it be?*

As a bonus, they would be rewarded with a picnic at the end of the journey, provided they brought their own food.

Tyler opened a jacket pocket to show her a sandwich. He winked. "There's another one just like it in my other pocket."

Zoey laughed. The guy came prepared.

The time came to climb into the raft. The thought flashed through her mind that she still had time to escape to the truck. She could wait there and read a book on her phone while Tyler went on without her. But she knew he would never leave her. He would stay behind with her, and she would feel guilty. The others were already heading for the raft and getting into the water. She looked at Tyler.

He must have sensed what she was thinking. "It's not too late to leave."

Just hearing those words calmed her. "No, I can do this."

"Are you sure?"

She gave him her most confident "yes."

Tyler smiled. "Then let's do it."

Soon enough, they were on their way down the river, heading into the foaming water. Zoey felt more alert than she'd ever been as she tracked the riverbank on either side and the raging water ahead. She clung to her paddle as they'd been taught, and she listened acutely to their guide for instructions.

As they bobbed and glided down the river, something strange happened. Zoey fell into the rhythm of responding to the flow of the river, paddling or not as the water and their guide dictated. She even grinned at Tyler during a calm stretch between rapids. She had never seen him look so happy.

Without warning, the guide shouted, "Get down!"

Zoey tried to brace herself on the rope handle, but her hand slipped.

Tyler reached for her hand, but when he let go of his rope, he was thrown from the raft.

Zoey panicked. *Stop. There's no time for that now.* Tyler was nose up, toes up as they'd been taught, but the water carried him farther away.

Zoey extended the T-shaped paddle handle to him while those beside her waited at the ready to help Tyler onto the raft. He reached for the paddle but narrowly missed it. He rolled over and swam toward the raft.

She reached out with her paddle again and slipped. Someone grabbed her jacket from behind and pulled it back before she could fall overboard. Tyler swam closer. Zoey gritted her teeth and stretched her paddle into the rapids for the third time. Finally, he grabbed hold. Zoey dragged him closer until a guy beside her grabbed Tyler's life jacket and pulled him up into the raft.

All Zoey wanted to do was throw her arms around Tyler and hold him, but there was no time. The guide was already shouting, "Forward paddle!"

The rest of the trip was a blur, except for a few

moments when Zoey's concerned looks at Tyler were met with a reassuring grin.

Back on dry land, Tyler took Zoey's hands. "Are you okay?"

"Me? I'm fine. You're the one who fell in."

"And you saved me. I'm more concerned about you. Have I scarred you for life?"

"No. It was strange. When you fell overboard, I panicked, but I knew I had to do something. So I set my fear aside. It was still there, but you were more important. I had to help you."

"Thank you."

"You don't need to thank me. I just did what I had to."

He grinned. "So you *do* care!"

Zoey blurted, "Yes. I didn't know how much until I saw you in the water, and I was afraid I might lose you."

Tyler drew her into his arms and kissed her on the forehead. "I don't want to lose you either." They gazed at each other, and time seemed to stop. Zoey wanted it to, but she also wanted it to keep going. She wanted him to kiss her. For an instant, she thought he might, but he sighed and took a step back.

His face brightened with the slightly mischievous expression she'd seen before when he wanted to ease tension. "I knew you'd keep me safe."

"Did you? That makes one of us. What if I hadn't?"

"I had a backup plan."

"You had a backup plan for falling out of the raft?"

"Well, not so much of a plan, but I've been rafting before. I was on the swim team in high school, and I was a lifeguard every summer through college. I know my way around water."

Zoey stared at him. "You are full of surprises."

"Don't get me wrong. Rapids are unpredictable and dangerous, so getting pulled back onto the raft was my first choice by far. But I kept an eye on the riverbank in case I needed to swim for it."

Zoey wasn't sure how to react. "That might have been some good info to share before you fell into the water and scared me to death."

"But then I wouldn't know how much you care."

Zoey wondered if he knew how much that soft light in his eyes affected her. It put her at a disadvantage, so she decided to keep it to herself. But the satisfied glint in his eyes that followed revealed it was already too late. It must have been written on her face.

Taking her hand, he led her to an empty picnic table. Before sitting down, he paused. "Hold on. I just need to check something." He reached into one pocket and pulled out a soggy sandwich. The bag dripped on the table. "I guess the watertight seal broke when I fell in. No problem. We can share the other one." He pulled it out of his other pocket. It was surprisingly dry but entirely mangled. He winced.

Zoey laughed. "Let's look for a restaurant on the way home."

"Great idea."

AFTER LUNCH AT A ROADSIDE STAND, Tyler offered to make dinner that evening. He just needed to stop for some groceries, and then they could head over to his place.

Zoey reached back and touched her hair to confirm that it was indeed damp. "I really need a shower to wash off the river water."

"Okay. I'll drop you off on the way home, and you can come by when you're ready."

"Brilliant plan, except I don't have a car."

"Oh. Right." He thought for a moment. "You can shower at my place."

When she hesitated, he suppressed a smile. "It's okay. There's a lock on the bathroom door."

"I didn't think—that's not... I..." She was hopelessly flustered.

"Let's just stop at your place. You can take a quick shower, and then I'll drive you to my place."

She was clearly relieved. "Okay."

When they arrived, Aunt Minnie was there to

greet them. While Zoey cleaned up, Tyler shared the highlights of their afternoon.

When he finished, he glanced toward the hallway and lowered his voice. “It was risky, taking her rafting. But I think she’s okay about it.”

“It was a big stretch for her.”

“I know, and it nearly backfired. But I just had a hunch.”

Aunt Minnie peered at him. “Or maybe you’ve gotten to know her. Your instincts are good.”

“What instincts?” Zoey stood at the door to the kitchen with dry hair, fresh clothes, and a light in her eyes that was captivating.

“Ready?”

“I think so.”

Tyler stood. “Good. I’ll give Minnie a break from my odious company.”

Aunt Minnie laughed. “I don’t know about odious. But definitely—”

“Don’t say it.” Tyler interrupted. “Just let me go on believing you adore me as much as I adore you.”

Aunt Minnie’s eyes twinkled as she looked straight at Zoey. “Get out of here.”

The pair burst into laughter. Tyler gave Aunt Minnie a kiss on the cheek then left with Zoey.

TEN

Tyler set down the grocery bag, opened a bottle of Merlot, and poured two glasses. "Would you like the grand tour? It's a quick one."

Zoey took the glass he offered. "I'd love it. So far, it's gorgeous."

He frowned. "I think you meant manly."

"It's that too. I mean it. I love log cabins, and it's definitely still got that rustic feel. But the finishes are clean and bold and remarkably tasteful." Zoey frowned. "That didn't come out right. I just didn't know you had that side to you."

"Really? So you basically had me pegged as a kind of ham-handed guy with dead animals and antlers on the wall, an ice chest in the corner, and a hardware-store bucket for a bathroom?"

She gave him an embarrassed smile because he

was on the right track. But she surveyed the kitchen with its matching appliances and polished concrete counters and saw how wrong she had been.

Tyler narrowed his eyes.

She shrugged. "How do I know you don't have an ice chest hidden in the pantry?"

"Good guess, but no pantry."

"See? That's what I get for assuming. Although I haven't seen the bathroom yet."

"By all means, follow me. You know, they make toilet seats that fit those hardware store buckets. This is a class operation here."

He wasn't serious. He couldn't be serious. Tyler led her into a bathroom with an actual toilet, a slate walk-in shower, and a sleek soaker tub under the window.

Zoey gasped.

That glint was back in his eye. "Disappointed? I probably have a bucket leftover from the renovation. I could go grab that for you." He took a step toward the door.

Zoey grabbed his arm to stop him. "It's stunning."

He looked duly proud of his work.

Zoey shook her head. "It's just... so impressive."

They meandered back to the kitchen area, which was at one end of the great room. There was no bedroom, just a large, open space with a vaulted ceiling and an imposing stone fireplace on the opposite wall from the kitchen. A massive log bed rested against the wall to the left of the fireplace, and a thick rug defined a sitting area on the opposite side.

Zoey caught sight of the entire wall of windows to the right of the fireplace. "That must be spectacular in the daytime."

Tyler nodded. "It's a pretty nice view. I'm planning to build a large deck out there this summer, but I'm taking a break from DIY projects so I can focus on my plastering career."

Zoey was enchanted—with the cabin and with how good it felt to be with Tyler. *I would love living here.* She nearly said it out loud but caught herself. She meant in a general sense, not with him. But that sparked a new train of thought. *What would it be like to live here?* That fluffy, quilt-covered bed looked inviting. She felt herself blush.

Tyler glanced toward the kitchen. "I'd better get cooking. I'm starving. Aren't you?" He went to the counter and pulled items out of the grocery bag. "I hope spaghetti's okay. It's the only thing I know how to cook—that and sandwiches."

"Spaghetti sounds great. Can I help?"

"How are you with salads?"

"I'm a genius at tearing lettuce."

"Great! Make yourself at home."

Zoey wanted to do just that. Along with an overwhelming attraction to Tyler, she felt comfortable with him. The underlying panic she'd grown to expect in dating situations was barely perceptible with him. He had a way of making her feel as though anything she did around him would be okay. He just liked her—the person she was when she let down her guard. She stole another glance at him as he browned the ground beef for the meat sauce.

He flashed her a roguish smile. "Hey, stop distracting me. This is a delicate process."

She grinned and turned back to her salad preparations. Warmth filled her chest. She'd heard people talk about pinching themselves to make sure they weren't dreaming. If she was asleep, she didn't want to know. She would live in this dream.

Dinner was delicious, although food was hardly at the forefront of Zoey's mind as they talked and laughed over dinner. Her life had had few perfect moments, but that was one she would always remember.

IT WAS all Tyler could do not to kiss her. He'd become fixated on her scent, on the satiny sheen of her skin, and the way electricity seemed to arc between them when they drew within inches of touching. To say it differed from anything he had known was an understatement. But that made it more of a challenge to keep the pace slow.

He counted himself fortunate to have worked up from hand-holding to hugging. When he progressed to a kiss on the forehead then the cheek, he began to have doubts—not of his feelings for her but of his self-restraint. When he'd kissed her on the cheek, their lips had been inches apart. A slight move and his lips would meet hers.

At the end of the evening, he pulled into Minnie's driveway to drop Zoey off. In one still, charged moment, he nearly did it—kissed her on the lips. But when they arrived at the door, the porch light came on.

"It's just the motion sensor," Zoey insisted.

Logic supported her explanation, but when he spied a sliver of light shining through a crack in the blinds, he couldn't help thinking of Minnie.

God love her—she could be looking out for her niece, although that's not Minnie's style. But once the thought planted itself in his mind, he couldn't get it out. So he hugged Zoey, wished her good night, and retreated to his truck.

So close. I came so close to kissing her.

Aside from a bit—no, a lot—of frustration, he was elated about his day with Zoey. She had actually fought through her anxiety out of fear for his safety. That was huge for her. It was huge for them. There was something between them that was special, but it was fragile. If he pushed her too quickly, he would lose her. He could not let that happen.

To that end, Tyler developed a theory. The more he saw her, the more comfortable she appeared. So all he had to do was make sure to touch base at least a few times a week—or, preferably, every day. The more he became part of her daily routine, the more likely she would be to give in to having an actual relationship. He was almost afraid to put it in words, but what he wanted more than that was a future with her.

AT FOUR IN THE MORNING, Tyler's phone rang. He reached an arm out from under the covers and groped about the nightstand for his phone. He found it but dropped it on the rug. It survived and kept ringing. He almost wished it had died so he could pretend it had never rung and go back to sleep.

"H—" Nothing came out. He cleared his throat and tried again. "Hello?"

"Good morning!"

"Murph." Tyler squinted and opened his eyes. "You know it's, uh, late... or early."

"Yeah, sorry. There's a story in Washington we'd like you to cover."

"Washington? Haven't you got people there?"

"Yeah, but none as good as you."

"Really?"

"No. But they're all busy."

"Thanks."

"There's a plane out of Albany at eight. Can you make it?"

"Yeah, I guess. There shouldn't be much traffic when I get on the road at... ugh, four thirty."

"Good. I'll send you your e-ticket by the time you're on the road."

Tyler groaned internally. "Great. You've thought of everything, haven't you?"

"Pretty much. So you'll do it?"

Tyler wanted so much to say no and go back to sleep. "Yeah, I'll do it."

He hung up. He might not need it yet, but he wanted the money. Murph was a friend but not so close a friend that he could blow off work opportunities without eventual consequences. If he said no enough times, Murph might stop calling. That was the trouble with the freelancing. If he wanted the money, he had to take the work when it came.

A half hour later, he pulled over to the side of the road in front of Minnie's house. With one glance at his watch, he knew he couldn't just knock on the door so early in the morning. It would scare Minnie to death, which wouldn't bode well for his future with Zoey. Plan B, tossing stones at Zoey's window, was unlikely to work as well as it did in the movies. She might call the police. He would have to use his one phone call to tell Murph he couldn't make it. He shook his head and pulled back onto the road.

Once he'd boarded his plane and taken his seat, he sent Zoey a text. Then he set his phone to airplane mode. He didn't know how long he'd be gone. Whether it was a day or a month, he was going to miss her.

ELEVEN

Zoey and Aunt Minnie sat at the kitchen table, sipping their morning coffee. Zoey was checking her email when her phone dinged with an incoming text.

It was Tyler. *I'm on a plane to DC for a last-minute job.*

She typed back almost immediately. *Oh. For how long?*

He didn't answer. She looked up at Aunt Minnie. "I just got a text from Tyler. He's flying to Washington for work."

"That's funny. He didn't mention it last night."

Zoey tried not to look too concerned. "It came up at the last minute."

"Oh, that's good, I suppose. He mentioned once that he wasn't sure what he was going to do work-wise. It sounds like he's solved that problem."

"Yeah, I guess so."

Aunt Minnie sipped her coffee as though she didn't have a care in the world. It was easy for her. She wasn't falling in love. "How long will he be gone?"

"He didn't say."

"Oh." From the look on Aunt Minnie's face, she had something on her mind. If she didn't choose to share it, it was probably better if Zoey didn't know.

A few minutes later, Aunt Minnie finished reading the news headlines on her phone and looked up at Zoey. "If you're not busy today, I've got something I need your help with."

"Okay." *Busy? I haven't got anything scheduled for the next several decades.*

They took her aunt's car to the theater, where Aunt Minnie had several swatches of fabric laid out on her desk. "I've come into some cash, so I'm going to put in new theater seats and hang new stage curtains."

Zoey's eyes widened. *Some money? New seats and curtains would cost... a lot!* "Wow! That's fantastic!"

"Isn't it? This place is really coming back together. Anyway, what I need help with is choosing the colors. If we're going with the original colors for the paint, we could stick with the deep red of the current curtains, but I was wondering about black."

Zoey thought for a minute. "I don't really know. Both would work. Why don't we go look at the space?" She had seen it thousands of times, but she'd never thought much about the curtains. They walked into the theater.

"Be brutally frank," Aunt Minnie said. "I want to know just what you think."

"Well... I think black might be good for the theater. Everything else up there is black, so black curtains would blend in and almost become part of the set."

Aunt Minnie smiled. "I agree."

Zoey's eyes swept over the space. "I just love it in here. You can almost hear echoes of songs, feet tapping out time steps, or the wartime newsreels."

Aunt Minnie looked over the tops of the orchestra seats at the stage. "And our family. They devoted themselves to this place. And now you're a part of it too." She shut her eyes, breathed in, then slowly exhaled. "Well, black curtains it is. I'll go make some calls, and we'll get that in motion."

Zoey wanted so much to ask her about the money. It wasn't any of her business, but she was curious.

TYLER WOULD BE GONE for a month. He stayed in touch. With some coaxing, he got Zoey doing video calls, so she got to see him on-screen. He asked her a couple of times to join him. After two weeks of missing him, she booked a flight to Dulles Airport in DC. Aunt Minnie offered to drive her to the airport. Zoey wanted to see Tyler so much, but when Aunt Minnie put the key into the ignition, Zoey said, "Wait."

One look and Aunt Minnie's expression turned serious.

Zoey stared straight ahead. "I can't."

"Honey, it's only an hour-and-a-half flight. You can do it. Tyler will be there when you get off the plane."

But what if he isn't there? She would be alone in a new place. Just imagining that made her panic. "I can't."

"You used to live in New York City. It can't be harder than that."

Zoey shook her head. "But New York City is different. I used to go to the city with my parents all the time. It was familiar. And when I moved there to teach, I knew my neighborhood. The shop owners knew me. Believe it or not, New York is like a bunch of small towns put together."

Aunt Minnie nodded. "But you've missed Tyler so much."

"I know, but I can't. I'm like a pot-bound plant."

Aunt Minnie spoke in a gentle voice. "A pot-bound plant just needs more room to grow."

"I can't. I'm sorry." She got out of the car, grabbed

her carry-on suitcase from the trunk, then retreated to her room.

She couldn't face Tyler in a video call, so she texted him. *I'm really sorry. I wanted to go, and I tried. But I couldn't.*

He was going to be so disappointed. It might tip him over the edge, and he would finally dump her.

He answered almost immediately. *That's okay. DC isn't going anywhere. We'll come back together some other time.*

She teared up when she read his reply. He was fine with it. He hadn't dumped her—not yet, anyway.

They made it through the next two weeks in their pattern of video calls and texts. Zoey stayed busy helping Aunt Minnie with theater business. She sometimes suspected her aunt was making busywork for her, but she didn't really mind. The work helped. She kept looking for a job opening, but there wasn't a lot of turnover in those small schools in the mountains.

Zoey sat in her aunt's office and leaned back in her chair. "I need some fresh air."

Aunt Minnie peeked out the lobby windows. "It's a gorgeous spring day. Go take a walk."

Zoey donned her sweater and left the office. Before she reached the stage door, it opened. Tyler walked in and held out one arm. The other was holding a three-foot-tall potted plant. She barely noticed the plant. She was so happy to see him, and she was transfixed by the light in his eyes.

With his free arm, he drew her against him and kissed her on the cheek. "Look at you."

She knew it was a compliment, but she wasn't sure what there was to look at. She was wearing her jeans, a comfortable shirt, and a broken-in cardigan.

He held out the plant. "It's for you."

Her eyebrows arched. Horticulture wasn't her strong suit, but she was sure Aunt Minnie would enjoy whatever kind of plant it was for her garden. "What is it?"

He looked downright pleased about it. "It's a cherry tree. I thought, since we missed the Washington cherry blossoms, we could plant this together." He scanned the bare, scrawny branches. "It's got to bloom eventually, right?"

Her heart felt a twinge of regret at that. She'd seen pictures of the lush and gorgeous blossoms. The trees would all be in bloom at this time of the year in DC. *It would've been romantic. Maybe next time.*

"Hey, what's wrong?" He bent over to set down the tree then peered into her eyes.

Zoey's heart ached. "I'm sorry."

He gently lifted her chin. "There's nothing to be sorry for."

That's not true. She couldn't get the words out, but he seemed to understand.

He looked insistent. "Nothing. Okay?"

"Okay."

His eyes softened. "I'm home, and we're together." He drew her into his embrace and held her.

AUNT MINNIE SHOOED them away for the afternoon. Tyler offered to take her out to lunch or the park by a lake, but Zoey said she would rather spend a quiet afternoon alone together. So they made sandwiches, went to Tyler's favorite spot by the falls, and caught each other up on the last month in DC and Cedar Creek.

It was peaceful and perfect. But Murph had been hinting about keeping him busy as a freelancer. It was exactly what Tyler had wanted when he'd moved there—a solid home base and assignments that wouldn't last more than a month. That was still a negotiating point he hadn't worked out with Murph. But in DC, his goal changed.

It was too early to center life-changing decisions around Zoey. But one day, he wanted to settle down in Cedar Creek with someone. He was hoping more and more that it could be her. He wanted a stable home life and family. Life on the road had worn him down. DC hadn't been his usual assignment, although it could have been as ruthless as some war zones. He felt like an outsider. He'd grown restless and caught up in a mindset he wanted to escape.

He'd made a mistake taking those freelance jobs from Murph. It was time to move on. *But to what?* That was something he would have to work out. He knew one thing he wanted—to spend more time with Zoey.

They spent his first day back doing ordinary things. They shopped for groceries to make dinner. Zoey cooked. He told her not to go to too much trouble, so she made a shepherd's pie. It was easy comfort food for a cozy evening. After dinner, they sprawled on the couch and watched a movie. By the end of the evening, they were tangled together in bliss.

As the movie ended, Tyler was a heartbeat away from planting a kiss on her that wouldn't end there. The bed was a few feet away. If he followed his desire, what came next could be what he'd dreamed of for weeks. Or she would panic and run, and they would never be the same. They had come so far, but they weren't quite ready—Zoey wasn't ready—for that.

Tyler hopped up. "I should get you home."

Zoey looked up, surprised and a little confused. "Okay."

He had her out the door and into his truck within a handful of minutes. She was silent the entire ride home.

As they parked in Minnie's driveway, Zoey finally spoke. "What's wrong? Just be honest. It's been a month. I know things can change. Feelings can change. It's okay. Just tell me the truth. I know I have some... anxiety issues, but I can take it."

"What are you talking about?"

"Come on. You pretty much gave me the bum's rush back there."

He knew he was slack-jawed, but he couldn't help staring. Worse yet, he couldn't find the words. He had to be delicate or at least find a tactful way to say it, but he sure couldn't think of one at the moment. So he looked straight at her and blurted, "I wanted to kiss you."

He cleared his throat. "No, that's not quite true. I wanted to kiss you and then take you to bed, which was right there. But I didn't want to push things or scare you away, so we had to get out of there because..." And then something came out that he wasn't expecting. "Because I love you."

He exhaled and shut his eyes. *Well, dammit, now you've done it.*

Zoey looked stunned, but he couldn't tell if she was thrilled or appalled by his words.

"I've been wondering why you never wanted to kiss me." Her voice was soft, and her eyes fell to her hands.

"What? Didn't want...? Are you kidding? I—"

For the first time in his career as a journalist, words failed him. So he gave up on speaking. He took her face in his hands, and he kissed her. Oh, *man*, did he kiss her. And she kissed him back until his heart felt close to bursting. Blood raced through every inch of his body. He'd known she could kiss from the diner incident. That memory had been partly to blame for his ongoing frustration. But the current kiss made the diner prank look like a warm-up. If she still felt nervous around him, her lips hid it well.

But when the kiss ended, she didn't say the words he longed to hear. The absence of those three little words sent him tumbling from the cloud he'd been floating upon.

Suddenly, the porch light flicked on, blinding and bright as the sun. *God love you, Minnie, but we could not have triggered the motion sensor from here.*

The light seemed to have brought Zoey back to her senses. With a glance toward the house, she climbed out of the car. "I'd better go."

Tyler nodded and walked her to the door, and she slipped inside with a whispered "Good night."

TWELVE

Zoey closed her bedroom door gently and collapsed on her bed. More than anything, she wanted to say the words. She did love him. She wanted to tell him. But saying it would have put things on a new level that she wasn't ready for.

She was ready for the relationship. She just couldn't face her fear of losing someone she loved. It wasn't a matter of trust. She believed in his love. But things happened. People died every day. They left home not knowing that a terminal illness, an accident, or senseless violence loomed around the corner. When Zoey had lost her parents, she hadn't thought she could survive it. She had, but she couldn't go through that again. Her therapist called it catastrophic thinking. She knew it didn't make sense, but logic couldn't cure emotions.

She had been through this before. None of her

relationships had worked out. Some had died a natural death, while others got to a point where the familiar sense of unease set in and led to the ultimate panic. Zoey knew herself. Years of therapy had at least given her that. She knew when to end things.

Except with Tyler. She had ignored all the signs because she'd been so happy, but with his confession, they were on dangerous ground. She was falling in love and didn't want it to end, so she would put off telling him until it was too late. He might not know it, but her heart was already his. That meant it was his to break.

Tyler would never intentionally hurt her. But no matter how much people loved each other, problems came up. Tyler had done everything he could to make it work so far. He'd even offered to fly her to DC so they could be together. She felt another twinge of regret at the thought.

It was time to be practical. It wouldn't last. Soon, Tyler would be off for a new job. He would want her to join him if the location was safe. When she said no, he would be understanding. He might not even object when she refused again and again. But their relationship wouldn't endure that indefinitely. When the newness wore off and reality set in, one or both of them would move on. Zoey didn't know when, but she knew it would end. It would only hurt more the longer she let it go on. It was past time to end it, and that broke her heart.

She tried to look at the positive side. She was lucky. It was a miracle, really, that the two of them on such different paths had arrived in the same place before veering off into other directions. She would never regret having known him. Later on, when she healed, she would remember how it felt to be with him and to be deeply in love. She would never feel like that again.

If only she was different. She wondered what it must be like to take risks and go to dangerous places. That was Tyler's normal, the polar opposite of Zoey's. But love was a powerful force. It had bonded them despite everything. If she could overcome her fear of commitment—her fear of losing him—there might be a chance to defy the odds and build a life together. But that was too big an if.

Zoey sighed in defeat. It was a distant dream. For someone with a clinical anxiety disorder, fretting over him was a recipe not only for a failed relationship but an emotional roller coaster that she could not handle.

I have to let him go. But she would always miss the passionate way he tackled life with a fearless curiosity and unbridled enthusiasm.

TYLER SANK into his leather chair and stared at the cold fireplace. *That was unexpected.* He'd told her he loved her because he felt certain that she loved him too. Apparently not. She'd left him hanging out there all alone with his "I love you."

What did you expect—that she'd throw her arms about you and declare her eternal love? No, but a simple "I love you too" would have been nice. He thought for a moment. That was definitely how it was supposed to work. Instead, he'd gotten silence and a big question mark.

He leaned back and rested his head. *I can't be that deluded. Nobody kisses like that without feeling something.* There had to be something else.

Why? Because no one can resist your charms? Accept it. She just isn't feeling it. It would be easy to pin her silence on her anxiety. But he couldn't blame every problem on that.

He kept mulling it over until he had revisited the same thoughts and insecurities. Nothing had changed. Nothing would until he talked to her and got her to share her true feelings.

Don't be an idiot. She won't unburden her soul just because you want her to. She obviously can't. Give her time. It was one thing to say that, but he'd put his heart out there, and she had more or less walked away.

Maybe he was the one who needed time. *Man, look at yourself. Take a break.*

THE FOLLOWING MORNING, he walked into the theater, chiding himself for not following his own advice.

Minnie looked up from her desk. "Tyler! What a delightful surprise!"

"How's the theater business?"

Minnie smiled. "It's good. Very good in fact." She narrowed her eyes. "But that's not what brought you here."

"No."

"Have a seat."

Tyler could see it on her face, but he asked anyway. "Zoey told you about last night?"

"Not really—just that there's something going on between you. I didn't press for more."

"I love her." He thought he registered pity in the old woman's eyes. But he hadn't come there for pity. He'd come for Zoey.

"Maybe you should tell her."

"I did. She just didn't... tell me."

"Oh."

Tyler gave her a knowing look.

Minnie leaned back and sighed. "I can't tell you what she's thinking or feeling. Although, if I had to guess, I'd say she's crazy about you."

He rolled his eyes, looking hopeless. "Yeah, I can tell."

"The thing about Zoey is... well, you know she's been through a lot."

"I know. And I get the anxiety. I've been—or I've tried to be—supportive."

Minnie nodded. "And she's got a solid support network. She's got a good therapist and psychiatrist. I've done my best to be there for her. She's come through some tough years, and she's in a good place now. She'll continue to deal with her issues. It's in her chemical makeup." She locked her eyes onto his to drive home the fact. "It's part of who she is. She's an amazing young woman." Minnie put a hand on her desk. "And if you ever hurt her, you'll answer to me."

Tyler could tell she wasn't kidding. "I love her. I love everything about her. I can take it—all of it."

Minnie leaned back in her chair. "But can she? This isn't all about you, is it? Not at the moment. If she cares for you the way I think she does, then there must be something else that she needs to work through." Minnie paused, looking thoughtful. "Have you ever done any gardening?"

"Uh, not really. I mean, I've done a little landscaping around the cabin. But what's that got to do with—"

"Relationships are like plants."

Are they? He forced a polite smile.

"You can't really see a plant growing, but they do. You can see it in time-lapse photography. But you can't time-lapse relationships. You just have to wait."

Tyler resisted the urge to roll his eyes, and his annoyance made him feel guilty. He adored Minnie.

They'd been friends before he ever met Zoey. But he didn't need analogies. He needed Zoey to love him. *Is that so much to ask?*

"I guess what I'm saying is," Minnie continued, "don't give up. If you love her, then be there for her."

Tyler was doubtful. "Isn't that how stalkers get started?"

She laughed. "I said to be there for her, not surveil her. I have a feeling you know what to do. You just don't want to do it."

"And that is?"

"Be patient."

Tyler smirked. She was right.

Minnie hesitated then added, "I do think you should talk to her soon."

That confused him. "So... be patient and wait, but go talk to her now?"

Minnie had a troubled look in her eyes. "Big picture—be patient. Small picture—there are things you should know, but it's not my place to tell you. I've already said too much."

That cryptic remark worried Tyler. Before he could respond, she said, "It's not in my nature to meddle, but I want you both to be happy."

The reporter in him urged him to press her for details, but he resisted. "I'll go talk to her."

Minnie's concern cast a shadow on her encouraging smile.

Tyler got up to leave, but he paused at the door. "Where is Zoey, anyway?"

"Getting groceries. I gave her my car keys and sent her off. She needed to get out of the house."

With a wave, Tyler headed to his truck. His first thought was to go straight to the grocery store. Cedar Creek only had one. *No, don't do it.* Minnie would be proud. He wasn't succumbing to his impatience. *I'll wait for her in her driveway. 'Cause that won't look too pathetic.*

THIRTEEN

Parked in Minnie's driveway, Tyler pondered how love had the power to move mountains and make fools. He certainly felt like one.

He tried to retrace their relationship to see where it had fallen apart. Everything had been moving along, albeit slowly, until he'd left town for work. Both times, he'd returned and noticed an adjustment period with Zoey before things felt normal between them. It got longer each time, but he couldn't decide whether that was because he was gone longer the second time or because they had grown closer and felt the separation more deeply. The cause didn't matter at that moment. It was the effect that was ruining their relationship.

Tyler didn't even like being away anymore. The old rush he used to feel on the plane as he embarked on each new assignment was gone. It wasn't as though he didn't still like the work. He loved it. He just didn't want to leave home anymore.

He wondered if working from home might help him fix things. He envied people who could do that. They could check their email from bed then, still in their underwear, make some coffee. They also wouldn't have to bother with showering or shaving before getting to work. *What a life!* Of course, the not-showering bit might be off-putting in a relationship—or maybe it was the test of true love.

Even with daily showers, working from home would be perfect. He would never have to say goodbye and go for weeks without seeing her. They would be together. He could think of nothing he would enjoy more than spending each day with Zoey, doing commonplace things.

He had more than an hour to daydream about that because Zoey never came home. She appeared to be out for the day. If he waited any longer, his behavior would cross over from devoted to desperate. He had to get moving. He shoved his phone into his pocket. *Yeah, I could call her, but she might not answer.*

And here you are in her driveway, denying her that as an option. He felt like a jerk. Forcing his presence on her was the wrong way to go, so he left.

When he got home, Minnie's empty car was parked in the driveway. Zoey was seated in an Adirondack chair by the door.

He stepped up onto the porch. "Hi."

"Hi. I was about to give up on you."

He scratched the back of his neck. "I've been in your aunt's driveway, looking for you."

A rueful smile passed over her face. "I can't stay long. I stopped on my way back from the grocery store. The frozen food's going to melt."

"You could put it in my freezer so we'd have time to talk." He didn't expect her to shake her head no.

"That's okay. I just stopped by because I wanted to tell you in person."

Tyler braced himself. *This doesn't look good.*

"This morning, I got a phone call."

Tyler waited.

"I got a job."

"Oh. That's great." He sighed. *Minnie knew.*

"Yeah, a friend of mine, Alice, just got a job at a private school in the city. Her principal sent out an email to the staff about a job posting. A teacher's husband just got transferred, so there's an opening. Alice told her about me."

"In the city." He tried to wrap his head around that. "It all happened quickly, then."

"Not really. It was while you were in DC."

"Oh."

He couldn't shake the feeling that if he'd been there, things might've been different. *But what would I have done? Talked her out of it?* He couldn't have done that. If he wasn't enough to keep her there, then that was it. It was her choice, and she'd made it.

"You never mentioned going into the city," he said lamely.

"I didn't. Since Covid, they've been interviewing via video conference calls. So that made it easy."

Tyler nodded, hoping to appear supportive—not that he felt it. But it was looking as though there was nothing left between them but being polite. "And the curriculum's okay? You won't have to teach Marxism?"

"As a matter of fact, that question came up in my interview. I said that I think we should teach it."

Tyler hadn't expected that.

"I just think we should teach it as history—along with its results. Spoiler alert—it doesn't work. Never has. I didn't put it exactly that way. I think what I said was 'We shouldn't be conducting social experiments on children by inculcating them with historically failed ideologies.'"

"And they said...?"

"'We'll call you.' More or less. They were really pleasant, but I just knew that was it. I'd lost the job. But I had this moment. It was like the raft—when you fell overboard."

She lost him.

Zoey went on. "I was scared, but this was more important than fear. I knew what I was risking, but I had to take a stand. If I didn't, I'd wind up in the same situation I was in before, being asked to teach something I was intellectually and morally opposed to. I couldn't live with myself if I did that."

"It must have worked." Tyler saw a glimpse of her passion for teaching and the strength of her convictions. Even if he wasn't in love with her, he would have still been filled with admiration and respect. At the moment, it made losing her to a job hurt even more.

Zoey nodded. "It did. I was stunned when they called." Then she sighed and looked at him as if it all justified breaking his heart. "It's too great a chance to pass up. It's only fifteen blocks from my old school and neighborhood. I sublet my old apartment, so I'll have to find a new place to live. But a lot of apartments have opened up since the pandemic scared off so many people, so it shouldn't be a problem."

Tyler heard words that he didn't care about. "Good."

It seemed like the polite thing to say, but it wasn't. It was painful. The fact that she seemed fine with it made it hurt worse.

"I'd practically be getting my old life back."

Your old life. Tyler couldn't manage any more smiles. He searched her eyes. "I didn't know that's what you wanted."

Zoey nodded, but her bright facade faded. "About last night—"

"That's okay." He shook his head a bit too

emphatically and held his palm up. It was irrelevant anyway. "I love you" didn't sound good as a solo.

She looked wounded, or maybe it was pity he saw on her face.

When she hesitated, he said, "Well, congratulations." He was pretty sure he'd just pasted the least convincing smile on his face ever. He glanced around, wishing he could leave, but they were at his place.

Zoey looked toward the car. "I'd better go."

"Right. Melting groceries."

"Yeah." She winced. "Goodbye, Tyler."

"Bye."

Zoey got in the car, gave him a weak wave, then backed out of the driveway.

She's good at that—backing out—of my driveway, our relationship... He could still hear her tires crunching over his driveway gravel as he walked inside.

And to think he'd wanted to talk. He wished that conversation hadn't happened.

FOURTEEN

Tyler sat at his desk and stared at the blank computer screen. He had never wasted so much time in his life. For two or three days, he moped around the cabin. One morning, he decided he needed to get his mind off Zoey, so he went for a hike around his property. Even outside, he thought about Zoey. Realizing it was the thinking that was doing him in, he decided to go back inside and bury himself in work.

Work had always been his go-to coping mechanism. It had never failed to distract him. But minutes later at his desk, an empty document stared back at him.

Man, look at yourself. There he was in the place he had rebuilt into the home of his dreams. It was a writer's paradise, and his time was his own. He had everything he'd always wanted. But at that moment, he wanted Zoey. Maybe that made him greedy, but he couldn't be happy without her.

Her sudden decision to leave made little sense. She had a job offer. He got that. But he didn't know she'd been looking for work in the city. Since she'd already given up her apartment there, he assumed she would stay in the Cedar Creek area. So the job in the city had caught him off guard. Wounded heart and all, he had to step back.

Above everything, he wanted her to be happy. But the job move was so sudden. He couldn't help wondering if he was the reason.

He pulled a small jewelry box from his desk drawer and stared at the engagement ring inside. He scoffed at himself. *You really have to miss some cues to go out and buy something like this for someone who's moving just to avoid you.*

Looking back, he could see they had always been on different tracks. He was foolish to wish that, at some point, their paths might converge. Tyler shook his head as though that would shake off the madness that seemed to have seized him.

For a fleeting moment, he thought about giving Murph a call. The last time they'd talked, he'd told Murph he wasn't available for any more assignments, but Tyler had a feeling it wasn't too late to change his mind. But that would make him a hypocrite for doing the same thing he thought was a step back for Zoey.

No, this was his dream. He had worked so hard to

attain it. Despite a personal setback, he had to look forward.

Unsure how he would do that, Tyler got up from his desk, grabbed his phone and earbuds, and sank into the sofa. He scrolled through the news headlines, looked at a couple of playlists, then settled on a podcast. Throughout his work on the cabin, he'd taken breaks to watch this guy's weekly videos on home renovation projects. They'd helped Tyler through a couple of tricky phases of his home renovation. Earbuds positioned, he put his feet up and leaned his head back on the sofa. Ignoring the video, he shut his eyes and just listened.

Now that's a sweet deal. Spend your time doing what you love, and then, once a week, post a podcast about it.

Tyler sat up and pulled out his earbuds. *Why didn't I think of that?*

He mulled it over then said it aloud. "Why *didn't* I think of that?" Of course, there had to be hundreds —maybe thousands—of podcasts. It wasn't what he'd call a sure thing. But if others could do it and make money, there was no reason he couldn't.

It would take time to build followers, but he had enough saved up to get by for another six months—or a year if he was frugal. In the meantime, he could pitch articles to publications and pick up some cash here and there. Although he wasn't a well-known entity to the public at large, he had a decent reputation in the business. He'd won a few awards and had some good contacts. Once word got around, he could build up that stream of income while he submitted work to publishers. But the best part of it was that he could do it from home.

He went back to his desk and opened his laptop. He had some research to do.

AUNT MINNIE WAS MAKING the morning coffee when Zoey walked in.

Her aunt looked up. "There's some mail on the table for you. I forgot to go to the mailbox last night, so I just went out and got it."

Zoey looked at the return address. It was from her new school. She opened the envelope and examined the contents then slipped the papers back inside. Her aunt joined her at the table while the coffee finished dripping.

"It's the contract and paperwork for my new job."

Aunt Minnie came over and squeezed her shoulders. "That makes it official."

"It does." At the moment, she wished her aunt wouldn't be so supportive. She wanted her—anyone—to tell her not to do it. But Aunt Minnie would never do that.

When she'd first gotten the offer, she'd been elated. But as each day went by, she had a nagging feeling she was making a mistake. It wasn't about Tyler. Or maybe it was. But even if he was a factor, she wondered if going back to the city and leading her solitary life was the best thing for her. When encountering stress, her knee-jerk reaction was always to retreat. It was easy to get lost in the city and be alone in a crowd. Ironically, it was the best place to avoid human contact, which wasn't the healthiest situation for her.

And then there was Tyler. She had pushed him away out of her own skewed sense of self-preservation. Since then, she'd wondered if it was one of those things she would regret for the rest of her life.

She looked at Aunt Minnie. "How do you ever know if you're doing the right thing?"

Aunt Minnie smiled sympathetically. "You don't. I mean, some things have simple right or wrong answers—don't rob a bank. Don't stab anyone." She gave Zoey a rueful look. "But the others? I don't know. You can only analyze things to a point. Sometimes, it just comes down to trusting your gut." She looked into Zoey's eyes. "Or your heart."

The coffee maker spluttered, and Aunt Minnie turned and poured coffee while Zoey's head, gut, and heart battled it out. It was her life. Right decision or not, she would have to live with the consequences.

Halfway through her coffee, Zoey got up. "I need to make a phone call."

A few minutes later, Zoey emerged from her room, stunned. "I just turned down the job."

Aunt Minnie didn't look shocked, but she didn't quite look happy either.

"I don't want to go back to my old life. I've been happy here in Cedar Creek with the people who matter to me. I want to build a new life—one where I'm not alone." The next words were hard—saying them out loud would make them real. "I love Tyler."

Aunt Minnie's eyes shone, but she didn't look as surprised.

But Zoey couldn't believe she'd gotten the words out, so she said it again. "I love him."

Aunt Minnie patted her arm. "If you drop me off at the theater first, you can borrow my car."

ZOEY PULLED into Tyler's driveway and got out of the car. He didn't see her right away. When he came out of the shed, he was busy hauling a couple of old sheets of plywood. When he spotted her car, he propped the plywood against the shed. He brushed his hands off on his jeans and walked toward her, his brow furrowed.

Zoey got out and met him halfway. "Hi."

She couldn't quite read his expression, but he didn't look happy.

"I turned down the job. I'm not moving."

He seemed guarded. "That's good—if that's what you want."

She nodded and tried to get out what she'd come there to say, but she was too slow.

Perhaps moved by the awkwardness of the moment, Tyler began talking. "I'm glad."

He didn't look glad. He launched into the sort of conversation a person might have with someone who hadn't just broken their heart. "So, what will you do now? I imagine your aunt can keep you busy at the theater. I love that place. It's a great space. You can feel the history in it. That's how I got to know her. I walked in to ask about it. I guess it was the reporter in me—"

"I love you."

Fear gripped her. It was the biggest risk she'd ever taken. And there she stood, vulnerable, terrified, and so deeply in love that she worried her heart would break.

He said nothing.

Zoey's stomach churned, and her heart ached. *Please say something. Tell me to leave. Something to put me out of my misery.*

Finally, he took a step toward her.

That was all it took. She flew into his arms, and he gripped her tightly. They clung to each other as though they might be pulled apart any moment. But Zoey knew there was no force that could rip them apart now—not even her fear.

Tyler pulled away just enough to lean down to kiss her. He said her name and held her, pressing his cheek to her forehead. He told her he loved her and kissed her again.

"I love you too," she said. "I have for a long time."

For all of her fear and uncertainty, Zoey finally felt peace. This was right. *They* were right. She and Tyler were where they belonged.

FIFTEEN

Aunt Minnie took off for Florida with no notice. She hadn't planned a vacation. One morning, she just asked Zoey to drive her to the airport. Tyler went along for the ride and insisted it was his turn to drive home.

Zoey stewed in the passenger seat over Aunt Minnie's sudden departure. "I mean, I guess she deserves a vacation. I don't remember her ever taking one. It just seems so unexpected."

Tyler smiled. "She's a big girl. She can handle herself."

"I know that." His lack of concern was a little frustrating. "It's just, you see things a certain way, then when they change, it takes an adjustment."

Tyler's eyebrows drew together. "It's a vacation, not a major life change."

Zoey nodded and stared out the window, unconvinced.

IN AUNT MINNIE'S ABSENCE, Zoey was in charge of the theater. It was nothing new for her. She'd spent years helping Aunt Minnie out, so she knew every aspect of the operation.

On her first afternoon off, Zoey headed for Tyler's cabin. When he invited her in, she was met with what had to be a dozen boxes in various stages of being unpacked. "What's all this?"

He beamed. "My new project!"

"New project?" Whatever it was, he looked like a kid on Christmas morning with a shiny new bike.

"I'm starting a podcast."

When Zoey first saw the boxes, several thoughts flashed through her mind. *Is he still moving in? Moving out? Fighting and losing an addiction to online shopping?* Podcast wasn't one of them.

He shrugged. "I'm a journalist burned out from the road, and I want to work from home. What better way than a podcast? Before you get too worried—"

"I'm not worried, just surprised."

"I'm developing multiple streams of income. I can make this work."

His enthusiasm was contagious. "I know you can."

"You don't think I've lost it?"

"No! I think you've found it."

Over the next several days, they shared the excitement of his new endeavor. Together, they tossed around ideas and mapped out a plan. In the midst of the process, Tyler stopped and stared at Zoey. "We're a really good team."

Her brow wrinkled. "Yeah. I thought we'd established that."

He laughed. "No, I mean working together. I can't do this alone. I was planning on hiring someone to operate the camera, maybe act as a producer and personal assistant. But I've got a better idea. Let's be partners."

Zoey thought for a moment. "I don't think you can afford me."

"We'd be partners. You'd produce, I'd perform. We'd build the business together."

"In that case, I don't think *we* can afford me."

The humor in her eyes faded.

"I can't ask Aunt Minnie to support me indefinitely. She's amazingly generous, but at some point soon, I've got to get a job—an income—and earn my own keep."

"We could still be partners. You'd just work part-time until the podcast gets off the ground. And if it doesn't within a reasonable time, I'll set you free." He winked. "But only professionally."

Zoey considered his offer. She liked the idea.

"Okay. It's a deal." She reached out her hand to shake on it, but he pulled her into his arms.

"Let's seal this deal with a kiss."

By the end of the second week of Aunt Minnie's vacation, they had built out, soundproofed, and had an electrician wire the storage shed, turning it into a home studio. Arm in arm, they stood and admired the finished product.

"Let's take her for a spin!" Zoey powered on the equipment.

Tyler didn't need any convincing. He sat at his desk, donned his earpiece and lapel mic, and sat poised to begin while Zoey manned the camera.

When she gave him the signal to start, he said, "Welcome to the pilot episode of *The Real Issue*. I'm Tyler Farrington, and I love Zoey Beckett. That's this week's real issue. Tune in next week, when *The Real Issue* will get up close and personal with Miss Beckett." He lifted an eyebrow. "Or maybe we won't wait until next week."

Zoey stopped recording and laughed. "You've obviously got a hit on your hands."

"As long as I've got you in my arms." He crossed the room to embrace her.

"Who writes your copy? It's a little corny."

"Oh, yeah? I'll show you corn. There's an entire field of it just down the road."

He scooped her up, carried her outside, then set her down.

Zoey lifted her chin. "Come on. Where's that cornfield you promised me?"

"It's a little farther than I remembered."

Zoey acted offended. "Are you implying that I'm too heavy to carry that far?"

Tyler winced. "Uh, no! Not at all! But I just remembered, it's spring. The seeds aren't even out of the ground."

She narrowed her eyes. "Not exactly a good save, but I'll take it."

Tyler wiped his brow. "Phew!"

AUNT MINNIE SURVIVED HER VACATION. In fact, she looked carefree when Tyler and Zoey picked her up at the airport. She chattered cheerfully on the way home about the warm weather and the therapeutic effects of the Florida sun.

She was so happy, in fact, that she insisted on taking them both out to dinner. It was there that she made her announcement. "I'm retiring."

Tyler was happy to hear it. Beneath all the shock, so was Zoey. She supposed her aunt must be in her midsixties. She was entitled to retire and enjoy some leisure time.

Aunt Minnie continued, "And I've bought a house in Florida."

"A house?" She'd had no clue her aunt had the

funds to do something like that. *And what about the opera house?*

"Well, a condo. It's a little sudden, I know," her aunt continued. "But I found a beautiful condo in Boca Raton. I'm not the retirement community type, so I thought I'd just get a condo with a view of the ocean. This place is perfect. I can sit on my balcony and hear the waves. And there's a guest bedroom in case anyone wants to visit."

While Zoey absorbed the news, Tyler said, "That's great."

"I know you must be wondering about the theater." She gave Zoey a sympathetic look. "It'll be fine, because I'm giving it to you."

Zoey's jaw dropped. "But—"

"I know. It's a little intimidating at first. I once went through the same thing. But it's a family tradition. And now it's your turn."

By that time, Zoey had closed her mouth, but she was still working through the shock.

Her aunt wasn't finished. "I know that there's work left to do, but I'll cover the cost of new seats and curtains."

Zoey felt light-headed. She not only battled confusion, but she questioned her aunt's cognitive status. "You can't! You don't have the money! I saw the bids. Forty thousand dollars for new curtains. And the seats. Those are close to a quarter of a million dollars! Aunt Minnie, that's impossible."

Aunt Minnie tilted her head and then nodded. "Well, yes and no. I've got a nest egg set aside."

"Set aside from what? Robbing banks in your spare time?" Zoey wished she hadn't said that. She hadn't meant to be rude and sarcastic, but her aunt had been struggling to make ends meet for years. The theater barely made enough to scrape by, and it only made that much because her aunt was so creative at generating revenue.

Aunt Minnie laughed. "No, I didn't rob any banks, but it does have something to do with currency."

Tyler must have sensed Zoey's head about to explode, because he put a reassuring hand over hers.

Aunt Minnie leaned back in the booth. "As you know, I've always been interested in technology, more so than most people my age. I've just always loved computers. I guess it came from typing all those papers in college. I was such a bad typist that I used to paint Wite-Out over all my mistakes. My papers shed dandruff when I turned them in. So when computers came along, they were like magic." She laughed.

Zoey marveled at how cavalier her aunt was. But she still hadn't explained her surprise nest egg.

Aunt Minnie's eyes sparkled as she continued her story. "A few years ago, I was at the dentist's office." She paused to point at her teeth. "Brush and floss. That's the best advice I can give you in life. Anyway,

I read a fascinating article in a magazine. It was all about a new world-changing concept called blockchain. I didn't understand it exactly. I still don't, to be honest. But it seemed revolutionary. So I did something crazy."

Zoey must have looked off, because Tyler squeezed her hand.

Aunt Minnie leaned forward and put her palm on the table. "You know I'm not a gambler. I don't even like bingo. But I had a good tax refund that year—nearly five thousand dollars. So I bought a new food processor and invested the rest in Bitcoin."

It was Tyler's turn to looked shocked. He regarded Aunt Minnie thoughtfully. "When was this, Minnie?"

"Oh... 2013? I think I paid about one hundred sixty a coin."

Tyler practically fell out of his chair. "But today, one Bitcoin costs—" He pulled out his phone and looked it up. "Sixty grand!"

Aunt Minnie shot them a satisfied smile. "Yeah. I didn't want to touch it until I retired, but I think I can afford to buy the theater some news seats and curtains, with enough left over to enjoy my retirement."

Zoey recovered enough to be thrilled for her aunt and grateful for the theater. Then it struck her. "But you're leaving us." Tears filled her eyes without warning. Aunt Minnie had been the only stable presence left in her life, and she was going away.

Aunt Minnie tilted her head sadly. "Only because I know you'll be okay."

Tyler put his arm about Zoey's shoulders. "You won't be alone." He looked at Minnie. "I'll take good care of her."

Aunt Minnie gazed at them warmly. "I know you will." She narrowed her eyes. "But you two had better visit!"

SIXTEEN

For the next several days, Aunt Minnie briefed Zoey on different aspects of the theater. They walked through everything from the filing system to the contents of the storage area under the stage.

Tyler stayed out of their way. He had plenty of work to do on the podcast. Friday came, and he needed a break. He suspected Zoey might need one, too, so he called and asked if she wanted to grab a coffee.

"There's a cleaning crew at the house. They're getting it ready to show. But we could meet at the theater."

"Actually, I was thinking of the coffee shop. They're trained professionals, you know. Besides, you'll be spending all of your time at the theater soon enough."

"Okay."

When Tyler had found out about Minnie putting her house on the market, Zoey had told him she planned to move into the theater's cloakroom until she could find an apartment. She assured him it would be fine.

"It's got old, tall windows that let in lots of light. It's actually bigger than my New York apartment."

Tyler was skeptical. "Minus the kitchen and bathroom."

Zoey dismissed that. "I can shower in the backstage dressing rooms, and I don't need much of a kitchen—just a microwave and my old college dorm room fridge.

Tyler frowned.

"You know what else it has?" she'd added. "Zero rent. That's a huge plus."

Zoey seemed happy enough with the plan.

He smiled to himself as he approached the coffee shop entrance. As soon as he walked in, he spotted her at a table near the window, her head leaning against the back of an overstuffed loveseat, earbuds in, eyes closed. *Good. She's relaxed.*

ZOEY'S EYES popped open to find Tyler sitting beside her.

She quickly pulled out an earbud. "Oh, you're here already!"

He pointed to her ear. "Must be a good song."

"It's my go-to playlist when I'm in a mood. It makes me happy. Here, listen." She handed an earbud to him.

They listened together to a cut from the soundtrack of one of her favorite movies. She suddenly realized that they were "that couple" in the coffee shop, heads together, foreheads nearly touching.

She lifted her eyes, now moist and shining.

"What's the matter?"

She shook her head. "I'm happy."

He smiled. "Why's that?"

She shrugged. "It's hard to say."

"Hard to say because you aren't sure, or hard to say because you *are* sure and just don't want to say it out loud?"

"The latter. I don't want to jinx it."

"Zoey." He looked in her eyes. "You're allowed to be happy."

She looked thoughtful. "Yeah, I guess I am."

With a nod toward the door, Tyler said, "This is where we first met. Remember?"

They shared a lingering smile.

Tyler took a deep breath. "There's something I need to tell you."

Panic ripped through her. Things had been going too well. Something was wrong. "You're sick?"

"What? No!"

"You're leaving me?" she whispered.

"No!" He frowned and struggled with his words. "So I just—I thought this would be the perfect place."

"It's... the only place for coffee. Except for the diner." Ordinarily, she might have dismissed it as a passing moment of confusion, but he was acting too strangely to ignore.

Tyler stood abruptly. His face lit up for no reason. Zoey followed his eyes as he glanced around the coffee shop. There was the usual assortment of people absorbed in their coffee, newspapers, and laptops.

When she turned back around, Tyler dropped to one knee.

"Ow! Dammit!" He glanced up at Zoey. "Sorry! Coffee bean." He pulled the bean from under his knee and tossed it away.

He rolled his eyes then shrugged helplessly. "This is not how I planned it, but—" He cleared his throat, drew in a deep breath, then exhaled. "Zoey, meeting you here in this coffee shop has changed my life. I'm hopelessly, desperately in love with you. I mean, look at me. I'm on my knee in a coffee shop. My kneecap has just sustained a blunt-force trauma from a rogue coffee bean. Please put me out of my misery and... Marry me. I mean... will you? Marry me?"

Indescribable joy filled her until she thought her heart might burst. She didn't know how long she'd sat there, but Tyler looked worried. Time had slowed down. He was waiting for her. She realized her head was bobbing ridiculously. "I love you!"

He still looked confused. "Sorry. It's the reporter in me, but just to be clear, that's a yes?"

She laughed. "Of course it's a yes!"

Tyler winced. "Oh, crap! I forgot. I should've been holding this." He reached into his pocket and pulled out a small box. His hand trembled as he struggled to open it, so he held it out to her. "You'd better take this and put it on. I might drop it."

She had never seen Tyler like this. For once, he was the one looking out of his comfort zone.

He loves me! She couldn't believe it was true. *He just proposed to me!* She slipped the ring onto her finger. It felt as though everything—all her anxiety and fear, the uncertainty in her gut that left her questioning everything, and the untethered feeling she'd had since she lost her parents—settled down. The world simply stopped in a moment of perfect equilibrium. For the first time in her life, she had found her footing. She was on solid ground in the place she was meant to be, with the person she was meant to be with.

She lifted her eyes to meet his. "Look at us."

Tyler's eyes shone as Zoey leaned down to kiss him. He caught her face in his hands and kissed her again.

The hairs on Zoey's arms began to stand on end. It had grown uncharacteristically quiet. There was no grinding coffee or whirring blenders. Then their lips parted, and the entire place burst into applause.

Zoey's cheeks felt so hot, they must have gone crimson, but she lifted her hand in an awkward wave.

Tyler glanced at Zoey's coffee. "Are you finished with that?"

Huh? We just got engaged, and that's your first question? "Yeah." She reached for the cup to hand it to him, but he took her hand and stood, bringing her to her feet with him.

"Let's get out of here."

Hand in hand, they walked past the smiling faces of bystanders who, for a moment, had stopped to witness two ecstatic people beginning their life together.

SEVENTEEN

On a sun-drenched April morning, Tyler and Zoey sat in a Paris sidewalk cafe. As they huddled together over a laptop, Tyler ceremoniously pressed a key.

"There. It's posted. Our podcast's one-year-anniversary episode." He grinned, closed his laptop, then slipped it into his backpack.

"Now, how about that stroll?"

The cherry trees were in full blossom as they walked alongside the bookstalls on the banks of the Seine. Now and then, they stopped to peruse a volume that caught their eye. In the gaps between the stalls, they glimpsed the long tourist barges that glided along the river.

Tyler pulled Zoey closer and planted a kiss on her forehead. "When we're done here, let's go to the Musee D'Orsay. There's a clock there I want you to see. Then for dinner, I've booked a dinner cruise on the Seine.

"Will we see the Eiffel Tower?"

His eyes twinkled. "You might miss it while you're gazing at me with those stars in your eyes, so we might have to save that for tomorrow."

"Tomorrow sounds perfect."

ON A BALCONY OVERLOOKING THE BEACH, Aunt Minnie stepped out in her gauze caftan, set down her iced tea, then stretched out on her cushioned chaise. After adjusting her floppy-brimmed hat, sunglasses, and Bluetooth earphones, she settled back to listen to the latest episode of her favorite podcast.

"Hello. I'm Tyler Farrington, and this is *The Real Issue.*"

Next from J.L. Jarvis:

From Edinburgh's enchanted cobbled streets to its misty hills, a timeless romance blooms.

The Red Rose

THE CEDAR CREEK STORIES

Welcome to Cedar Creek—where the mountains are quiet, the seasons change with grace, and love finds its way back to hearts that need it most.

IN THE HEART of the Adirondacks lies a town where healing begins, friendships are rekindled, and love takes root when you least expect it.

. . .

FROM A SNOWBOUND CHRISTMAS that brings two weary souls together... to a wedding that reunites childhood best friends with unfinished business... to a summer of unexpected love between two people carrying heavy pasts—the Cedar Creek series is a tender journey through heartbreak, hope, and the kind of love that rebuilds what life has broken.

PERFECT FOR FANS of Robyn Carr, Debbie Macomber, and RaeAnne Thayne, this emotionally rich, feel-good trilogy proves that sometimes, the place you go to escape is exactly where you're meant to be.

jljarvis.com/cedar-creek

THANK YOU!

Thank you for reading! If you enjoyed this book, please consider leaving a review or a rating. Your feedback on bookstore, Goodreads, and Bookbub websites helps other readers discover books they'll enjoy.

THANK YOU!

Thank you for reading! If you enjoyed this book, please consider leaving a review or a rating. Your feedback on bookstore, Goodreads, and Bookbub websites helps other readers discover books they'll enjoy.

BOOK NEWS

Sign up for the J.L. Jarvis Journal for exclusive benefits, including free books, special offers, exclusive content, and updates on new releases: news. jljarvis.com

BOOK NEWS

Sign up for the J.L. Jarvis Journal for exclusive benefits, including free books, special offers, exclusive content, and updates on new releases: news. jljarvis.com

READING ORDER

Waterfront Summers

(Can be read in any order)

The Cottage at Peregrine Cove
The House on Serenity Lake
Moonlight on Mariner's Bluff

Drake & Wilde Mysteries

(Reading Order)

#1 *Love in the Time of Pumpkins*
#2 *Secrets in the Hollow*
#3 *Shadow of the Horseman*

Standalones

(Can be read in any order)

A Kiss in the Rain

App-ily Ever After

Once Upon a Winter

The Red Rose

Highland Vow

Short Stories

(Can be read in any order)

Seasons of Love: A Short Story Collection

The Eleventh-Hour Pact

A Christmas Yarn

The Farmer and the Belle

Work-Crush Balance

Cedar Creek

(Can be read in any order)

Christmas at Cedar Creek

Snowstorm at Cedar Creek

Sunlight on Cedar Creek

Pine Harbor

(Reading Order)

#1 Allison's Pine Harbor Summer

#2 Evelyn's Pine Harbor Autumn

#3 Lydia's Pine Harbor Christmas

Holiday House

(Can be read in any order)

The Christmas Cabin

The Winter Lodge

The Lighthouse

The Christmas Castle

The Beach House

The Christmas Tree Inn

The Holiday Hideaway

Highland Passage

(Can be read in any order)

Highland Passage

Knight Errant

Lost Bride

Highland Soldiers

(Reading Order)

#1 The Enemy

#2 *The Betrayal*
#3 *The Return*
#4 *The Wanderer*

American Hearts

(Can be read in any order)

Secret Hearts
Forbidden Hearts
Runaway Hearts

For more information, visit jljarvis.com.

Get monthly book news at news.jljarvis.com.

ABOUT THE AUTHOR

J.L. Jarvis is a left-handed former opera singer/teacher/lawyer who writes books. She now lives and writes on a mountaintop in upstate New York.

jljarvis.com

www.ingramcontent.com/pod-product-compliance
Lightning Source LLC
La Vergne TN
LVHW020044110826
845155LV00029B/631

9781942767466